95

A Circle in Time

A Circle in Time

Peggy Dymond Leavey

Peggy Dymond Leavey

Napoleon Publishing

Cover art: Patty Gallinger
Book design: Craig McConnell

The poem *Kubla Khan* quoted from on page 15
is by Samuel Taylor Coleridge (1772 - 1834)

Napoleon Publishing
a Division of TransMedia Enterprises Inc.
Toronto, Ontario, Canada

Printed in Canada

05 04 03 02 01 00 99 98 97   5 4 3 2 1

Canadian Cataloguing in Publication Data

Leavey, Peggy Dymond
        A circle in time

ISBN 0-929141-55-5

I. Title

PS8573.K2358C57 1997   jC813' .54   C97-931329-5
PZ7.L42Ci   1997

For my children
Jeff, Tim and Christine.
For Corinne, Kandy and Chris,
and for Mom.
Love and thanks.

Chapter 1

I was twelve years old already and not a single interesting thing had happened in my entire life. Unless you counted the birth of my twin sisters, which I didn't. But that was before that Saturday last November when the strangest thing happened. Afterwards, everything was different.

On that particular Saturday, Dad's regular helper, Dennis, was home with the flu and, although Dad had said he could manage by himself, (he was, after all, only on a scouting mission), I offered to go along. It was either that or stay home with the sitter as if I too were only seven years old.

"Better put that extra hard hat on before we go inside," my father advised when we arrived at our destination and I hopped down from the truck into the bitter wind that blew off the river. While Dad adjusted the plastic strap inside the hat so that it would fit my head, I studied the building we were about to enter.

Known only as the Studio, the building hadn't been used for anything for a long time. It was too costly to maintain as a vacant building, and now the Heritage Committee had lost its fight to save it. It was scheduled for demolition at the end of January. Dad and I were here today because he was looking for some special molding for a renovation project he was doing for a local doctor.

"You back again, Jim?" A man with a clipboard greeted Dad at the door and followed us into the building. "Say, didn't you have your name down for one of the old filing cabinets? Looks like we'll be able to start clearing that stuff out the first of the week." He smiled then at me. "Who's your new assistant?"

"This is my eldest daughter, Wren," Dad said, and I felt the gentle pressure of his hand on the top of my hat. "Don't let her size fool you, though; she's pretty good with a crowbar."

Already, several people were looking around the main room, examining the panelling on the walls, measuring the window frames. One man was concentrating on scraping a bit of paint off each one of the doors, and a woman was counting the squares of embossed tin on the ceiling while her husband kept track in a notebook. The sharp smell of old dust and mouse droppings filled my nostrils.

In spite of my father's compliment about my skills, we weren't using a crowbar on anything today. Dad had a sample of the molding he needed to match, and I helped him to compare it with the wood trim around the doors and windows in this room and down the hallway. None of it was the same as Doctor Shuman's.

"It's close," Dad decided, "but I'd like to get Dennis' opinion." Instead, he bought two wooden coat racks from a jumble of odd furniture which sat in the middle of the room.

The man with the clipboard waved us outside with them. "No reason why you can't take those with you today," he said. Dad and I carried the racks out to the truck, setting them on their sides in the back and pulling the tarp up to cover them.

I stepped aside to let a wine-coloured car pull into the parking space beside us. A woman got out, juggling her handbag and a stack of yellow papers. "This is a sad day for Trenton, I must say, Mr. Ferris," she said, directing her comment at my father.

I recognized her from her pictures in the newspaper. Mrs. Widdicombe was one of the people on the Heritage Committee. "I've brought some flyers to leave here for anyone who is interested," she said, trying to straighten the flapping papers. "The Committee has arranged for a showing of *No Sunrise in the Trenches*, the last of the movies that was made here." She shoved a flyer into my hand before she moved indoors to speak to the others.

"What did she mean, Dad, the movies they made here?" I asked.

My father batted at the dust on the arms of his coveralls. "This was a movie studio, Wren. In the old days. I thought you knew that."

"It was? You mean, like the movies you see at the show or on video?"

"Yep. Real movies. Come on now." Dad hauled his tool box out from the back of the truck. "I want to poke around inside a bit more, see if there's anything else I should speak for."

I hurried behind him, trying to hold the sheet of paper flat enough to read. "They'll be showing the movie at the high school cafeteria, November eleventh. Could we go? Have you ever seen any of the movies they made here, Dad?"

"It was a little before my time, Wren." He held the door open for me again. "I can remember hearing stories about a famous director who was here, though. Donald Donaldson, the one who made that *No Sunrise in the Trenches.*"

"That's the one they're showing!"

"Well, it's an old one," Dad remarked. "Must go 'way back to the Twenties."

"1927, it says here."

"That Donaldson fellow created quite a stir when he was in town, or so I've been told. He was a very important person, back in England anyway. When he came here, he even had his car shipped over, a big shiny affair with wire wheels and a chauffeur to drive it. Said it had belonged to the Prince of Wales. Pretty big-time for our town."

I looked around with growing interest at the room where we now stood. As long as I could remember, this building in the middle of Trenton had been vacant, with the windows on the ground floor painted over, as if they had secrets to hide, and the outer doorways collecting bits of wind-driven garbage. But this wasn't just any boring old building. Important directors had come and gone through its doors, most likely real movie stars too.

"Okay if I look around?" I asked as Dad waited to talk again to the man with the clipboard.

"Most of the interesting stuff has gone now." The man spoke without looking up. "We had some real souvenirs—some original show bills, even some of the tin cans they stored the reels of film in."

He took some money that was being offered to him by a young man holding a pair of dilapidated folding chairs. "There's a big stage across the hall there, two storeys high. You might want to take a look at that. And you can still see where the dressing rooms were, behind the gallery upstairs. At least, for the moment you can. Someone's spoken for those stairs already."

I scurried away while I could.

"You be careful up there, Wren," Dad called after me. I was already halfway up the narrow iron steps to the next level, my hand against the brick wall to steady myself.

"Sure, Dad. Just call me when you want to go." I looked over the railing into the depths of the naked stage below me and then up to the network of ropes and steel beams above. The ceiling was hidden somewhere up there, in the dark.

The rooms across the hall from the gallery which overlooked the massive stage were disappointing. I'd hoped to find rows of lights over the dressing tables, lots of make-up bottles and racks of fancy costumes, the kind of behind-the-scenes view I'd seen in magazines. None of those things were there now. I could only imagine what it might have been like. The empty walls were all the same shade of dirty yellow, the paint scarred where fixtures had been removed. The small windows let in a minimum of late afternoon light.

Several sections of a long mirror had been torn off the wall, and I moved through the room to where one remained, mottled and cracked, the last in the line which must have stretched the length of the make-up table.

I dusted its surface with my hand, thinking of the actors and actresses who might have gotten ready to play their movie roles in front of this mirror. I'd seen pictures of early film stars—women with hair in row after row of tiny little waves, single curls glued to their cheeks, mouths like red valentines. And dreamy-eyed men with sad smiles.

My own pale, angular face stared at me bleakly through the grime. My sharp nose with its smattering of freckles, the safety hat which came down almost to my eyes, my untidy brown hair that no one could do anything with, sticking out in all directions underneath. No one was going to mistake me for a movie star. I drew a perfect oval around my face in the film which coated the glass. If I had the power to change my reflection, I thought, I'd give myself large, luminous eyes set widely apart over a perky, turned-up nose, and curly hair the colour of wheat.

Suddenly, without my having heard anyone approach, I saw in the mirror that there was someone behind me. A man. I turned around quickly, but to my surprise, no one was there. The room was empty. Sunlight flared for a moment through the windows. Had my eyes been playing tricks on me? I turned back to the mirror again.

Someone was reflected there. He was wearing a soft, cloth cap of a beige tweed material that sat at an angle over deep-set brown eyes. Heavy eyelids drooped at the corners, and deep lines ran past his mouth to his chin. It was a sad face, rather than one that would frighten me. He just stood there, motionless. And then, while I stared, the figure faded and became nothing.

Dad was waiting for me at the foot of the stairs. "Ready to go, Wren? I was just about to give you a shout."

"Come with me a sec, Dad?" I caught his hand, my heart still thumping hard in my chest. "I want you to come and see something."

He must have sensed the worry in my voice because he clattered with me back up the narrow stairs. "What's this all about, Wren?"

I drew him into the room. "It's the funniest thing, Dad. There was a man in the mirror, standing behind me. Here, in the dressing room. But when I turned around he wasn't there."

Dad squinted skeptically into the glass. The only reflections in the mirror were our own. "The mirror's old, Wren," was my father's explanation. "Look how the back's showing through in places. You might have seen a shadow of that."

"It was so weird, Dad. It really looked like a man's face."

"Whose? Someone from downstairs? I shouldn't have let you come up here alone."

I shook my head. "I've never seen this man before."

"Well, there's no one here now." He lifted the cuff of his coveralls off his wrist and checked his watch. "It's almost four, so we'd best be off. We have to pick your mother up. Her car's still in the shop."

Suddenly, I was seized by an impulse. "Could we buy the mirror, Dad? Please? They want to get rid of all this stuff anyway. Maybe we could even take it with us today?"

"What would you want this for? You can see it's cracked, and look, this corner is right off."

"For a souvenir. So that I could say I had something from the Studio. It's all going to be gone in a little while. Seriously," I pleaded. Dad was studying my face, looking a little puzzled. "I'd really like to have it."

He gave in. "It isn't worth a whole lot," he said. "Let's see what they want for it."

I kept my fingers crossed that it wouldn't be much, and it wasn't. The man with the clipboard let us take it away, surprised anyone would even want it.

When we left the building together a few minutes later, I was carrying the mirror under my arm. Just then the sun came out again, breaking briefly through the curtain of clouds that had hidden it for most of the day, bathing the gray walls of the old Studio in rosy light. For me, it had become a magic place.

Chapter 2

Dad steered the truck along the curb in front of a large brick house in one of the oldest parts of the city and stopped. The houses in this neighbourhood were as big as the trees, with verandahs and sunrooms, lots of angles to the roofs and numerous chimneys.

"She must be rich to live here," I decided, peering out at the house behind the low stone wall and the perfectly trimmed cedars which lined the front walk. Light spilled out onto the tidy lawn, cleanly raked of autumn leaves.

"Old money," Dad yawned.

This was the home of my mother's newest client. Mom has a business which provides help to elderly and shut-in people, allowing them to stay in their own homes. She runs errands for them, fixes nutritious meals and generally keeps them company. We could see my mother now, standing in the window of a front room, her coat on, waiting. She waved when she saw the truck, and a few seconds later, she came out to join us.

"What have you got there?" Mom asked as I slid over to make room, and she eyed the object in my lap. We'd wrapped it with a piece of old blanket Dad had found behind the seat. I lifted the covering to show her the mirror.

"Hmm. What are you going to do with that?"

"It's a souvenir," I said. "Part of Trenton's history."

A few drops of rain spattered on the windshield. "How was your new client?" Dad asked as we headed down the hill towards the bridge and home across the river.

Mom sighed. "It really is pathetic how grateful these people are for a bit of attention. This lady's name is Mrs. Bain, and she's just about the sweetest, loneliest old dear I've ever worked for."

Dad reached over to touch my mother's cheek. "How about stopping to get a pizza for supper, Val? I think we're all bushed."

"Suits me," Mom agreed.

"Double cheese," I suggested, being helpful.

For a while, Mom and I sat without speaking and watched the other cars move through the parking lot of the pizzeria. I was still feeling a little peculiar, other-worldly almost, after my experience at the Studio.

"Your dad find the molding he wanted?" Mom asked finally, without lifting her head from the back of the seat. Her face, looking pale and tired, was spotted with the raindrops on the windshield.

"Not exactly," I said. "He bought some funny old coat racks, though. Everyone was looking at stuff. It really was a cool place, Mom. Did you know they used to make movies there? No one ever told me that before. Don't you wish you could have been around then?"

I saw her smile. "It was a long time ago, Wren. I think its heyday was between the two World Wars." She shut her eyes. "I can't imagine where you're going to put that mirror. You have a perfectly good one in your room."

"Maybe we can put it inside my closet door. I know it isn't in very good shape."

Dad was back. "Watch, it's hot on the bottom," he warned, handing the fragrant box of pizza through the window and going around to get in on the other side. I inhaled the steam and the mouth-watering aroma of oregano and cheese. Dad started the engine and the wipers swept across the windshield, bringing the lights of our small city back into focus. Our next stop would be home, the two-storied house with the peach-coloured trim on Edgeview Crescent.

My twin sisters were sprawled on the floor watching television, but they scrambled up quickly when they saw the box Mom slid onto the table. "Pizza, yippee!"

I set my mirror down on the kitchen counter and dug out the spray bottle of window cleaner from the cabinet underneath. I was hoping that a little polishing would improve its appearance before it drew any more criticism.

"What's that ugly old mirror for?" one twin asked, coming to the sink to wash her hands and wrinkling her small nose at her wavy reflection.

"It's for my room, if you must know."

"But it's cracked."

"I can see that."

"There's a corner off of it," said the other twin. "And it looks kind of rusty." I glared at them and they backed off, going to sit at the table with my parents and the pizza.

When the twins were born five years after me, my parents went all out and named them Genevieve and Jennifer. They have pink cheeks with matching dimples and naturally curly hair. Dad says it reminds him of the colour of sunshine, like Mom's. He doesn't seem to notice that hers is mostly white now.

There are worse names than Wren, I guess. I heard about a girl in a book who was named

Scout. My parents' big mistake had been in letting my mother's father choose my name. He'd waited through the births of five grandsons for a girl and said he didn't know how much time he had left. My grandmother had been in the Women's Royal Naval Service in England when they met. She had been the WREN.

❧   ❧   ❧

Dad and I decided that the best place in my room for the old mirror was over my desk where there was a small shelf which helped to cover the missing corner. Now, every time I glanced up from my homework I would see myself and the backwards writing on the poster which hung behind me on the door of my closet.

"In Xanadu did Kubla Khan
A stately pleasure dome decree;
Where Alph, the sacred river, ran
Through caverns measureless to man
Down to a sunless sea."

I was doodling one evening at my desk, copying the backwards letters from my poster, and thinking I could write a secret message for my best friend Dawn to read, something she had to hold up to a mirror to decipher, when I was startled to see a strange girl standing behind me.

I looked quickly over my shoulder to see who had come into my room, but there was no one there. It was happening again! Just like the time before when I'd seen the reflection of the man, the girl was there when I looked again in the mirror.

I was alone in the house at the time, so I couldn't call anyone to come and confirm that what I was seeing was real. I turned from the room to the mirror and back again several times, but it was always the same. There was no one else in the room. But there definitely was someone in the mirror.

She looked to be about my age, maybe a little younger. She had pale, clear skin like fine china and smooth, brown hair that hung evenly just below her ears. Her brown eyes looked enormous in the small, white face. She wore a navy cardigan sweater, and the collar of a white blouse was turned down neatly over it at the neck. She was pretty, in a fussy sort of way, as if someone insisted she keep tidy all the time.

She stood too close behind me for me to see the rest of her in the mirror. Like the man I'd seen before, she didn't move but was as motionless as if she were the reflection of a painting. Then, very slowly, the image faded and was gone.

This was definitely spooky. Who were these people? I knew they weren't optical illusions caused by the poor condition of the glass or a part of the backing showing through, as Dad had suggested.

Too shaken to stay up in my room, I retreated downstairs to turn on every light in the house and wait until the rest of the family came home. Genevieve and Jennifer were suitably impressed by my story, although my mother warned me not to frighten them with my wild imagination.

"Do you want me to take the mirror down?" Dad asked, clearly puzzled.

"Not really," I admitted. It was as if I were drawn to it, mesmerized by it. Besides, there was nothing menacing about the two figures I'd seen. Instead, they both wore rather sad expressions. But who were they? And why were they appearing to me?

I did decide to cover the glass with a towel from the bathroom before I climbed into bed that night. I didn't like the idea of being watched while I slept. And I kept the door open.

I had to remember to uncover the mirror in the morning. Otherwise, I knew my mother would insist that I was frightened and that the mirror had to be removed for my peace of mind.

I couldn't wait to tell my best friend, Dawn Rosen, about all of this the next day at school. We usually walked around together at recess till the bell rang. Sometimes one or two other girls would join us, but this recess I wanted Dawn all to myself. Dawn and I didn't have many secrets we didn't share, and she was a little ticked that I hadn't told her about the man in the mirror at the Studio.

I tried to shrug it off. "When it only happened that one time, I guess I convinced myself that I had imagined it."

"Oh my gawd, Wren! How can you be so calm?" She yanked up the sleeves of her jacket. "Look at my arms! Just look at them! I'm all goose bumps, it's so scary!" Dawn has what Mom calls "a flair for the dramatic." It's natural, I guess. Her mother is the head of Trenton's amateur theatre group.

"It wasn't scary, exactly," I said.

"Are you kidding? The minute you said those words, 'someone was standing there watching me,' I totally freaked! Okay if I come over after school?"

Standing over the desk in my bedroom, Dawn slurped her can of pop noisily though a straw. "What you saw had to be a reflection of something," she decided.

"I know that would be the logical explanation," I said. "But a reflection of what? And there's nothing logical about this. I really did see those two people. But only in the mirror. And they were both perfect strangers."

"It's weird." She inspected the glass, touching its cool surface. I'd done it a million times myself. "Looks like an ordinary mirror. Kind of old, though. Do you think it'll happen while I'm here?"

"I'm not sure."

Dawn tucked her hair behind her ears and determinedly settled herself in my chair, never once taking her eyes off her reflection. "I hope it's the girl who appears. I'd feel much better about having a kid in the room."

We waited. Nobody appeared, of course. Mrs. Rosen finally ended our vigil by insisting Dawn had to eat dinner at home with the rest of the family. And, no, she would not be back later. Wednesday nights she had Hebrew lessons.

The old mirror gave me no further surprises after that. As the days passed and no one else who wasn't actually in my room appeared in the glass, I began to take its presence for granted. I even put a few knickknacks back onto the shelf in front of it. Its shoddy appearance still bothered my mother, however. I found her in my room one day, peering critically at her reflection. "I've heard you can have these things refinished," she said, "but this isn't even a good piece of glass."

I made her promise she would never touch it.

"Maybe Daddy can put a frame around it for you, then. Cover that broken corner."

"No, Mother! I want it left just the way it is."

It was on the night we were to see *No Sunrise in the Trenches*, and I was getting my math homework out of the way, that the little girl appeared again. Would anyone else be able to see her? I had to know. I could hear the twins playing in their room next door. Cautiously, I rapped on the wall. I heard giggles and they rapped back.

"What do you want, Wren?" Jennifer called when I knocked for the second time.

I fixed my eyes on the girl in the mirror, willing her to stay. "Come here," I called softly to my sisters. "Come into my room."

It was an invitation they rarely received. I heard the bed bump against the wall next door, and the twins rattled down the hall.

"Quiet!" I hissed. They tiptoed into my room. I saw their eager faces behind me, reflected in the mirror. The strange girl had vanished.

"She's gone." I flopped back in my chair and

tossed my pencil onto the desk.

"Who's gone?" They looked around at the empty bedroom.

"Oh, no one," I sighed.

"You're weird," Genevieve decided. And they left me then to wonder whether or not she might be right.

Chapter 3

Mrs. Widdicombe, swathed in plum velvet, stood at the front of the high school cafeteria and looked mournfully out over the sparse gathering. Obviously, not everyone in town was as excited about this as I was. "On behalf of the Heritage Committee, let me express my appreciation to those people who have not forgotten that the movie industry was an important part of our city's history.

"We are grateful to the National Film Archives for sending us a copy of the movie on video tape. We are lucky to have it, in fact. Many of the earliest films have deteriorated past the point where they can be shown. Many more were destroyed in the 1960s when the warehouse where they were being stored caught fire." The speaker took a determined breath.

"This is Trenton's movie as much as anyone else's. If you watch closely you may even recognize a familiar face or two. A number of local people had bit parts in the picture, and I understand there are even a couple of you here tonight. Could I ask you to stand, please?"

Everyone craned around to have a look at the two elderly people Mrs. Widdicombe introduced from the audience. They stood briefly and we all clapped. They certainly didn't look like movie stars anymore.

"I know that one chap," Dad whispered, as a man with a full head of snowy white hair sat down again. "He does a bit of gardening for Dr. Shuman."

"I'm sure there are several among our senior citizens who were involved in the making of this film who aren't with us tonight," Mrs. Widdicombe went on. "My own uncle, God rest his soul, remembered working in the film company's carpentry shop, making sets for the indoor scenes. When we watch one of the early movies, we sometimes forget that someone had to build those props or paint that backdrop.

"Anyway, let's get on with our film. More memories are bound to be sparked by watching this historic epic." The large television screen flickered to life.

No Sunrise in the Trenches was a war movie, the story of a group of Canadian men who enlisted in a Highland regiment and went to fight in the trenches in France in World War I. The film followed the lives of three of the soldiers and the families they left behind in this country.

By the restless shuffling of the audience around me, I could tell that I wasn't the only one who had to stifle a giggle at the jerky way the actors moved in the picture. Maybe that was just the way the cameras worked in the 1920s. The film wasn't meant to be funny; the theme of the movie was very serious.

There was no colour and no sound, except for someone who was playing the piano in the corner of the cafeteria. Mrs. Widdicombe had told us the pianist would be playing the original musical score. In the early days, she'd said, the musical accompaniment had helped to drown the noise of the projectors in the theatres, as well as set the mood for each scene; but the man at the keyboard now speeded up and slowed down in all the wrong places, so we might have been better off without any music at all. He didn't look old enough to have ever played for a silent movie.

The dialogue was printed on the screen between the scenes in fancy lettering. At first, you could hear people in the audience reading it out loud and other people "shushing" them. The actors often seemed to have more to say than just the written words, making me wonder what had been left out. They spoke too quickly for me to try to read their lips.

All in all, it was a long movie. We definitely should not have taken the twins. They began to fidget and poke each other, and Dad had to separate them by sitting between them. Jennifer complained, a little too loudly, that she hadn't known it wasn't going to be a cartoon, and Genevieve fell asleep across three empty seats.

At the end of the movie, after the last of the actors had tottered away into the distance, arms about each other's shoulders, muddy kilts swaying, we read an on-screen announcement that the director, Donald Donaldson, would address the audience. First, a shot of the Union Jack, the British flag ("Ours too, at the time," Mom said), then Donald Donaldson appeared on the screen. The minute I saw him my mouth fell open in a gasp and stayed that way. I read his words without absorbing their meaning.

"Ladies and gentlemen. It has long been my intention to make a film about Canada's contribution to the war, to pay tribute to her many unsung heroes, the ordinary soldiers. It has been a story left untold. Until now. I think you will agree that after this picture there need be no further film about the war. *No Sunrise in the Trenches* says it all." Slowly, the picture faded to a blank screen.

Dad stood, stretched, and began distributing our jackets to us. "Always heard he was a bit of an egomaniac," he muttered.

But the cause of my amazement was not what he had said, but the face of the great man himself. I'd seen him before. Donald Donaldson was the man in the mirror in the dressing room.

"Are you sure?" Dad asked as we edged our way out around a cluster of people who were staying to chat, out into the frost-filled air where our breaths mingled with the exhaust of the departing cars.

"Absolutely. It was him!"

"Well, you know, that just might make sense." Mom steered a pair of sleepy twins ahead of her. "There was probably a picture of him behind you on the wall at the Studio."

"But there wasn't," Dad and I countered in unison.

Could images become fixed in old mirrors? I pondered this idea as I lay in bed that night. It was an interesting theory. But if that could happen, there should be hundreds of faces in that old glass. Instead, there seemed to be just two, unless I was in for more surprises. I knew now who the one was. But who was the little girl who had appeared to me on more than one occasion? I didn't get to sleep very early that night, not until I had made up my mind to do everything I could to discover her identity.

It seemed to me that a good place to start was with the man Dad had recognized in the audience at the high school. Maybe someone who had been around the Studio in the old days could shed some light on my mystery girl. If the face of the man I'd seen was Donaldson's, perhaps he was connected in some way to this other apparition.

Saturday found me at the front of Dr. Shuman's residence. The doctor's house was an imposing place with a brass-trimmed front door, painted deep red, and a circular driveway made of brick. His offices were in the back of the house. He'd been our family doctor forever and had delivered the twins seven years ago. On their worst days, I had trouble forgiving him for that.

To my delight, as soon as I walked up the driveway I spotted the elderly, white-haired man I was looking for. He was working on hands and knees cleaning up what had been, earlier in the season, beds of flowers. The basket he was filling was overflowing with dried iris flags and faded mums. He looked up when he saw me and rocked back on the heels of his rubber boots.

"Are you looking for someone?" he inquired. His voice was deep and pleasant.

"You, actually," I admitted. "My family and I were at the movie they showed at the high school last week."

"Were you indeed? And what did you think of it? Pretty good, eh?" He began slowly getting to his feet, each movement accompanied by a small groan, until he was standing upright.

"Well, I'd never seen a silent movie before," I said.

"In that case, I wish you could have seen it when it premiered. There was a full orchestra at the Odeon here, and mobs of people. It was really something."

I felt it probably needed more than a full orchestra, but I didn't say so. Undoubtedly, movie-making, like a lot of things, had improved over the years.

The man pulled off his muddy gloves and extended a hand. "Alfred Hopkins," he smiled.

"How do you do, sir. I'm Wren Ferris."

"Nice to meet you, Wren. Now, that's an unusual name. How d'you spell it?"

"With a W. Like the bird," I said.

Drawing a pipe out of one of the pockets of his work jacket, Mr. Hopkins went to sit on the stone steps. He held a match in cupped hands over the bowl of his pipe. He didn't seem to object to my company, so I sat down beside him. "I've always liked this house," I said, looking up at the ivy-covered walls. "Dr. Shuman is our family's doctor."

"You don't say. This here used to be a tourist home, you know. Best place to stay between Toronto and Montreal. Called it the Flutterbye Inn. Get it? Flutter by and stop in? Of course, that was before the Doc bought it." He took the pipe from between his teeth. "Now, what was it you wanted to see me about?"

"I hadn't realized anyone who lived in Trenton had been in the movies," I said. "That totally surprised me."

"Oh, there were quite a few of us, really. And that movie you saw wasn't the only one made here. Just the biggest. An 'epic', they called it."

"Do you remember the man who directed it?" I asked.

"Donald Donaldson? Of course. Who could forget him?" He tilted his head towards me and spoke in a conspiratorial tone. "D'you know he stayed right here in this house when he was in town? Now, isn't that a coincidence? He and his wife and his little girl and her English nanny."

"He had a daughter?" This was more than I'd hoped for.

Mr. Hopkins clamped his teeth over the stem of his pipe again and spoke around it. "Forgotten her name."

"How old do you think she was?"

"Just a kid, I guess. Maybe about your age? They brought her nanny over with her. I wasn't much more than a kid myself. Had a job after school at the hardware store. That's where the movie people saw me. Said I'd be perfect for this German soldier they were casting." He leaned forward, resting his elbows on his knees. "Oh, I remember those movie people, all right. Got all excited about the snow up here that winter, they did. Never seen anything like it. Bought skis and skates and toboggans like there was no tomorrow."

He gave a short laugh. "And coonskin coats too. Remember those? No, I guess you wouldn't. My, what a sight they were in those coats! Anyone who had one could sell it for any price to one of the movie people."

After a pause to suck on the pipe, he continued. "That Donaldson was a very difficult man to work for. I was glad I had only one week of shooting. He kept firing people, then having to hire them back on again when he found he couldn't do without them.

"He went through a pile of money too, making

his movie. Half a million dollars, they said. In those days, that was an awful lot of money. Ran up bills all over the place. Even had a chauffeur to drive him around town."

"And his little girl?" I reminded him.

"Oh, they say he was crazy about her. So I guess he couldn't have been all bad, could he? Terrible lonely life for a child, though. Brought her here to be with him and then spent all his time working. Dorothy!" He gave his corduroyed leg a slap. "Now that was her name. Dorothy."

Mr. Hopkins set the pipe down on the stones and got slowly to his feet, rubbing the small of his back with both hands. "Oh, those were high old times, all right. But old D.D., that's what we used to call him, you know, he made a lot of enemies." He indicated the house with a nod of his head. "Left this place here without paying the bill, even. He had no money in the end. Paid off some of his creditors with paintings. He was an artist too, you know. Cousin of mine owned the dry goods store in town. Mr. D. settled his bill there with one of his paintings. Not much my cousin could do. I have the painting now. Pretty nice water colour of some place in England."

"Well, at least you have that," I said.

"Oh, sure. But back in 1927, I imagine people would rather have had the cash. You can't eat paintings, you know." Alfred Hopkins started to work his hands back into the gloves. "Well, I'd best quit my jawing and get back to work. We don't often get warm days like this in November. Gotta make hay while the sun shines, as they say." His thick white eyebrows came together in a worried frown. "I guess what I told you isn't exactly what you wanted to hear, Wren Ferris. 'Fraid I wasn't exactly a fan of old D.D.'s."

"Oh, that's okay," I assured him. "I was just curious about him, is all. And about Dorothy, his little girl. What happened to her, do you know?"

Mr. Hopkins shrugged. "No idea. You could ask around, I suppose. There's still a few people hereabouts who worked for Donaldson during the filming. Though you'll find most of us are pretty old."

"Maybe I should ask my Gramps what he can remember. He's lived here all his life."

Alfred Hopkins smiled. "Well, there you are then. But don't be too disappointed, little bird. Everyone's busy with their own lives these days. Look at how they stayed away in droves from the showing of the movie last week."

Then, as an afterthought, he said, "You know, it's a good thing there are people like Mrs. Widdicombe and her committee. Otherwise, there'd be nothing left to show today's generation where it came from. No one's interested in the past anymore. Funny that a bit of a kid like you would be."

Chapter 4

After meeting Alfred Hopkins and learning that Donald Donaldson had had his daughter with him during his stay in Trenton, I was convinced that the little girl I had seen in the old mirror was Dorothy. She looked enough like her famous father that I was sure it had to be.

There seemed to be no pattern to her appearances. Days would pass without my seeing her. On other occasions she'd be there every time I looked up. But only for a moment or two. Then she'd vanish. I'd almost given up trying to get anyone else in the house to confirm my visions of her. So far, it just hadn't worked that way.

When our Grade Six teacher, Mrs. Morrissey, announced that our next project, due right after Christmas, would be one on local history, I knew right away what my topic was going to be. I seemed to have been given, without my asking for it, an inside track on the story of the days when movies were made in our city.

A few days after my talk with Alfred Hopkins, one of my mother's elderly clients happened to lend her an old newspaper, dated Wednesday, July 11, 1917. My mother brought it in to show me after school on Friday. I was in my room, trying to decide where to begin my project.

"It's very fragile," Mom cautioned. "But you might see if there's anything here about our movie industry." She spread the fraying pages on my desk. "This would be about the time the Studio was being built."

This early edition of the Trenton Herald was filled with photographs of citizens of bygone years—large families posing on the steps of wide front porches and grim-faced men with magnificent mustaches at town meetings. My careful search was rewarded by a small story about an actress from New York who would be starring in the next picture to be made in Trenton. Inez Weston had come to inspect the new movie studio and had declared it to be perfect. She was "weak with the anticipation" of working there. Other luminaries from the business were expected to follow.

Carefully I refolded the delicate pages. I had yet to talk to my grandfather to see if he remembered the years when they were making movies here. Maybe now would be a good time to call him. I pushed back my chair and started to get to my feet to phone him when something caught my eye. I dropped back down again at once.

There in the mirror, standing somewhere over my right shoulder, was the little girl. Without taking my eyes off the pale, serious face, I spoke to her aloud. "You're Dorothy, aren't you?" For an instant, I actually thought I saw her eyelids flutter.

"Your father was the director of *No Sunrise in the Trenches*." Could that be the beginning of a smile? I plunged on. "You came to Trenton with him. With your mother and your English nanny."

Nothing happened. Well, what did I expect? I was lucky she was still there. Of course, she couldn't hear and would disappear as she always did when I looked behind me. Very slowly, I turned my head.

She was wearing a plain, loose-fitting, gray dress that fell straight from the shoulders and was pleated from the knees to the hem, gray woollen stockings and shoes that fastened over the instep with a single, round button. She really was there. Behind me. In my room.

"Dorothy?" I whispered, gripping the back of

my chair with both hands, expecting her to vaporize at any moment. "Dorothy Donaldson?"

She reached up then and ran a hand over her smooth hair. It was a smile. As I continued to stare, I realized that we were no longer in my bedroom but facing each other in another room, one I remembered being in once before. It was the dressing room on the second floor of the movie studio. From somewhere outside came the sound of many excited voices.

"I knew you'd come," Dorothy said, speaking for the first time, her voice high-pitched and excited. "Daddy said he'd find someone for me to play with."

I looked around me, and the noise of my pounding heart filled my head. "I know where I am," I admitted slowly, over the din. "But I'm not sure how I got here. Or why."

"To keep me company, of course, silly. Now, come on, don't just stand there. I want to show you something." Impatiently, Dorothy seized my hand. Hers was soft and warm, and she drew me towards the window. "Just listen to them all down there."

When I could finally stop gaping at the real, flesh-and-blood girl beside me, I saw that what she was showing me was a crowd of people gathered outside, at the front of the building.

They were mostly men, but there were some younger women too, and small children, some of whom were perched on their parents' shoulders. Everyone was dressed in heavy winter clothing, the colours as drab as the time of year.

"They've heard that Daddy's looking for extras for a crowd scene," Dorothy explained breathlessly. "I don't think I've ever seen so many people all in one place."

Below us, someone was in the doorway, shouting through a megaphone, which was all we could see of him from our vantage point. "Be here at six-thirty sharp," the speaker barked. "We'll take all of you for this scene. There'll be a truck to take you to the location. Same pay as usual, dollar a day."

The megaphone then disappeared inside and, after a moment or two, the crowd began to break up.

"It's like that every time Daddy puts out a call for extras," Dorothy said. "Everyone wants to be in his film."

As the people moved away, I looked out at the city beyond, and what met my eyes was quite a different city from the one I'd been used to seeing all my life. I recognized the square, red brick building which housed the Herald across the street, with the trees on the mountain behind it naked now in late November, the stone church on the opposite corner. These things were the same. But there were not as many buildings facing us on the main street as there should have been. There were unfamiliar empty spaces between the shops, and there were several wooden houses that didn't belong there. No one actually lived on the main street anymore. This older street looked narrower, with no pavement or parking meters, no traffic lights at the corner, and the few cars that I could see were the boxy, old-fashioned variety, like the ones I saw whenever we had a parade.

There were billboards too, between the shops, with strange advertisements for liniment and Lux Laundry Soap and for the "steady heat of Pocohontas Coal, at twelve dollars a ton." If people were clamoring for parts in Donald Donaldson's movie, and we were heating our homes with coal, then I had definitely left the 1990s behind.

Dorothy was pulling at my sleeve. "Come on. Let's see if we can find Daddy." It was obvious that she thought it perfectly natural for me to be here. "I want to thank him for finding you."

Finding me? My mind was full of questions I hadn't had a chance to ask, but I followed Dorothy anyway, to a narrow flight of stairs behind a curtain at the far end of the dressing room. I had to concentrate on my descent because the stairway was so dark.

"We'll pop into his office and surprise him," Dorothy said over her shoulder, both hands brushing the walls on either side.

The small office at the foot of the back stairs was deserted. "Oh, fiddlesticks!" said Dorothy. "Well, never mind. We'll find him." Determinedly, she led me to a hallway which ran east and west the width of the building. A series of closed doors faced us. "He's probably in here," Dorothy whispered, and opening the first door, we stepped inside.

We were standing in a courtyard surrounded by what looked like farm buildings and facing a low structure with a tiled roof. A sign over the door announced that it was the "Three Ducks Café." Light streamed out onto the stones of the courtyard from the two curtainless windows. There were people inside, and I could hear laughter and music. Dorothy pushed open the door and we entered the little café.

"Cut!" someone roared.

Immediately, all the patrons in the restaurant swung around to stare at us. Now I could see, on either side of the café walls, banks of floodlights and high above us, the rows of black curtains which hung over the stage. We had come through a back door, straight onto the movie set.

The stunned silence lasted only a second before a figure came lunging at us from out of the shadows behind the floodlights. My first impression was of a big, brown bear. "Dorothy! What on earth!"

"Daddy!" Dorothy cried happily.

It was Donald Donaldson. "We're filming here, my pet," he explained, becoming immediately less agitated. "I'd just ordered everyone off the set."

"Sorry, Daddy," Dorothy chirped. "I've been looking for you everywhere."

Patiently, her father guided her off to one side and I followed, not knowing what else to do. Donald Donaldson crouched down in the shadows and took Dorothy's hands in his. "You really cannot stay, my dear. Perhaps another time. Nanny really should not have brought you here. I cannot imagine what she was thinking."

"She didn't, Daddy. She was busy. Mummy has one of her sick headaches, you know."

With an enormous sigh, the man rose to his feet. "I'll have Michaels take you back up to the house." Then, as if seeing me for the first time, he added, "Your little friend can go with you. I'm sure you will be careful not to let your play disturb your mother." He turned then and snapped his fingers in an impatient gesture.

Things were happening too quickly for me, and just as I was about to say I couldn't possibly go home with Dorothy, the scene vanished as suddenly as it had appeared.

I was alone. Dorothy and her father and the film crew were gone. I was back in my bedroom, my senses reeling. My history project was spread out on the desk in front of me.

It took several minutes for me to bring my everyday surroundings back into focus again. What had happened just now? Had I really gone to the set of Donald Donaldson's epic movie? Or had I only imagined it? But it was all so real.

I knew I had to talk to someone about this. I found my father planing boards in his workshop in the basement. He listened politely, his safety glasses pushed up into his graying hair, while I told him about the amazing thing I had just experienced. "It probably only lasted about ten minutes," I said.

My father, looking thoughtful, started to sweep the workshop floor very slowly.

"So?" I asked. "What do you think?"

"Honestly?" He leaned on the broom, his chin on his hands, an impish grin on his face. He must have thought I was teasing him. "I'd have to say you had a dream," he said. "A very vivid one, but a dream, nonetheless. Now, don't look at me that way. You have to admit it's pretty strange, Wren." He swept the pile of shavings towards the dustpan I held for him against the floor.

"But, Dad! I can tell you absolutely everything about it. The studio, the movie set, the film crew."

"Dreams are like that sometimes," he said.

"Maybe you're not going to bed early enough, dear," was how my mother later interpreted it. "You need to get more sleep."

Chapter 5

I was still puzzling over my apparent travel backwards in time, wondering if I'd ever be able to do it again, when the opportunity I'd been waiting for came—the chance to question my grandfather about his memory of Trenton's movie era. If he'd lived here all his life, he was bound to have some recollection of it.

It had snowed in the night. The first snowfall of the season had dumped several centimeters onto the city before the weather cleared. The twins made the first tracks around the house after lunch on Saturday. There was enough snow to make a respectable snowman, and I helped my sisters push one into shape around the front yard. I was hoping for a real winter this year, like the ones I'd seen in pictures of the "olden" days, with snow banks halfway up the utility poles and houses buried to their window sills. More and more I found myself wishing I'd lived in those more interesting times.

Genevieve was looking for some stone buttons for the front of our creation, and Jennifer had already gone inside to dress for a birthday party, when Dad appeared and began to clear the driveway.

"When I get this done," he announced, pulling his toque down over his ears, "I'm going to run over to Gramps' place to make sure he's able to get out. You want to come with me? I have to drop the twins off at the birthday party on the way." I didn't need to be asked twice.

My mother set a stack of clean laundry into my outstretched arms as the four of us left the house. "Tell Gramps we'll be over next week to put up his Christmas decorations," she said. The twins were already arguing over which one of them was going to carry the present.

Grandpa Ferris is the only grandparent we have who lives close enough for us to visit. We only get to see our "down east" grandparents, my mother's family, in the summer holidays. At 88, Gramps still keeps his own house, with a little help from us and some of his neighbours.

To my disappointment, Gramps was asleep when we arrived. He often napped in the afternoon. When Dad discovered that the house was locked, he set about to clear the driveway without even knocking on the door.

"Shouldn't we wake him, Dad?" I suggested, hopefully.

"Not yet, Wren. You get the broom out of the back seat. I'll do the shovelling."

By the time his driveway and sidewalk were clear, Gramps appeared at the front window in his old gray sweater coat, waving at us to come in. We sat in our wet boots, our feet on the newspapers Gramps spread under the table, drinking the sweet tea he insisted we needed "to take the chill off," and eating the cookies Mom had sent.

The table in Gramps' kitchen is always set. The only time the cloth gets changed and the little gift jars of jam returned to the fridge is when Mom comes to fetch his weekly laundry.

He and Dad always have some business to discuss when they get together. Dad looks after his father's banking and letter-writing, so all those details have to be gotten out of the way first.

"I'm doing a project at school, Gramps," I began as soon as I thought it polite to turn the conversation to myself. "I need to talk to you about the olden days."

"Just how 'olden' would that be, now?" asked Gramps, and I saw him trade winks with Dad.

Dad got up to pour himself more tea from the enamel pot on the back of the stove, and topped up Gramps' cup while he was on his feet. "Wren's discovered quite an interest in Trenton's history," he said. "Been asking a lot of questions about the time they made movies here. What do you remember about it?"

"Well, that was a long time ago," the old man said. "A lot's happened since then. Now let me see." He studied the transparent skin on the back of his hands while he thought about it. "Well, I remember when I was a kid what a novelty it was for us to have the movie people here in our town."

"Then you used to see them, Gramps? Like, around?"

"Oh, they were around, all right." I tried to be patient while Gramps held his teacup with both hands and moved it to his lips, where it clinked gently against his teeth as he sipped.

"Us kids used to go and watch them filming all the time," he continued. "If one of us saw the people from the Studio setting up their cameras somewhere, we'd tell all our friends, and before you knew it, there'd be a couple dozen of us on the street corner. Rubber-necking. We followed them whenever we could."

"That must have been fun," I said.

"It was fun, all right," Gramps agreed. "They shot movies all over town—on the street corners, the mountain, the banks of the river. Never knew where they were going to be next. Sometimes they got mad at us, told us to move along."

"How old would you have been when all this was happening?" I asked.

"Well, they built the Studio here near the end of the Great War and made a few pictures," Gramps remembered. "So I was just a kid then. There were five or six little movie companies who moved in and made a picture or two. Always had high hopes, they tell me, and always ran out of money. The place was deserted much of the time I was growing up."

"But what about Donald Donaldson?" I prompted. "You wouldn't have been a kid when he came to town."

"No, that's true. When he arrived to make his big picture, I was a young man. Place got pretty busy in the Twenties. The province took over the Studio and made government films here, documentaries. All kinds of 'em. And then, the next thing you knew, the newspaper was full of stories about Donald Donaldson coming. The company that got him to write and direct a movie here figured it was going to put Trenton on the map. And for a while it did. Gave work to a lot of people too, people who needed it."

I reached for another cookie. "So it was a good thing, the movie business?"

"For some, yes, it was. People came from all over the country to see if they could get a part in the movie."

"What about you, Gramps? Didn't you want to be in it? I know I would."

"Well, not me, exactly," Gramps smiled. "But, you know, your grandmother did. So-o-o, smitten as I was, I went along with her. We were both in it, if the truth were told."

My father set his cup down so quickly that the tea slopped over into the saucer. "You never told me that, Dad!" he choked.

"Really, Gramps?" I hiked my chair up closer to the table, leaning on my arms, eager not to miss a word. "How come you never told us?"

"We were just extras, child. Just extras. They hired a bunch of us young people to be in a scene which was taking place in a fancy ballroom. And oh, were we young." He paused, the smile deepening the wrinkles around his pale, blue eyes. "First and only time most of us had ever worn evening clothes."

"What did you have to do, Gramps, in the ballroom scene?" I prodded.

"Oh, just mill about, talk to each other, dance

a bit and drink coloured water," Gramps said. "Look like we were having a good time. Your grandmother loved it."

"And did you see yourselves in the movie? After it was finished?"

"You know, we never did," he admitted sadly, "and that's the part that bothered your grandmother."

"Why?" I asked. "What happened?"

"They cut a lot of the footage, and that's probably what happened to the part we were in. The picture was far too long, I heard. Anyway, we went to see the film when it came to Trenton. It played here for a couple of weeks at the Odeon Theatre, but your grandmother and I could never find ourselves. She was pretty disappointed."

"No wonder," I sympathized. "But what about Donald Donaldson, the director? Did you ever get to meet him?"

"Oh, I remember him, all right. He was there, directing the scene, although I never spoke to him or was introduced to him personally. He stayed up at the Flutterbye with his family, he did. Little daughter too, I heard, with her English nanny. But we never saw the child, of course."

Gramps unhooked his wire glasses from around his ears with trembling fingers. Dad was beginning to make noises about how he thought we should be leaving. I think I might have been able to persuade him to stay a little longer, except that the phone rang. It was Jennifer, saying that they were ready to go home.

"Funny, what you can remember when you put your mind to it," Gramps muttered, coming to the door to see us off, his slippers scuffing on the linoleum. "Can't say as I remember what I had for breakfast, but I remember those movie people from all those years ago."

I paused, halfway out the door. "Anything else, Gramps?"

"Now, I have to think a bit, child."

Dad was trying to ease me outside. "Don't wear your grandfather out on the first try, Wren," he cautioned. "We'll talk again."

"It'll keep till next time, Gramps." I leaned over and kissed the soft, dry skin on his cheek. My grandfather was not much taller than I was these days. "I have to find out everything I can about it for school, you know."

"I'll put my thinking cap on," he promised. "Your grandmother now, she'd have been the one to tell you about it. What a great memory that girl had!"

I remembered something then myself. "Mom said to tell you we'll be by to put up your

Christmas decorations next week, Gramps."

"I didn't think I'd bother about them this year, child."

"Why not?"

"Just a waste of time for an old man like me. Someone only has to come and take them down again."

"Come on now, Dad," my father urged. "You don't want us to get in trouble. The twins especially are looking forward to doing your decorating, so you and I had better not argue with them."

"Better not tell them you ate so many of my cookies, either," muttered Gramps, holding the front of his sweater coat together. He closed the door and we heard the key turn in the lock behind us.

Chapter 6

The sound of my mother's voice calling my name reached me from the foot of the stairs. I had been lying on my bed daydreaming, my hands behind my head, wondering more as each day passed if I'd only dreamed my visit with Dorothy Donaldson at the movie studio.

"You coming or not?" There was a hint of impatience in my mother's question. Had she asked me this already?

I went to the head of the stairs. "Do I have to?"

"I suppose not." She was buttoning her old winter coat. "We're taking the twins to get new boots before the stores close."

"Then I'll stay home."

"We won't be long." The front door slammed.

I returned to my room, leaning against the door and letting it close behind me. Out of habit, I sat down in front of the mirror and, to my surprise, discovered that Dorothy was already there, waiting for me. "What took you so long?" she asked, pouting.

It was late afternoon, cold and raw. We stood at the edge of a dirt road which was rutted and slippery with mud. It was the wrong time of year for fireworks, yet as I looked around me at this strange new scene in which I found myself, only seconds after deciding not to go to the mall with my family, the sky suddenly lit up with explosions of light. Again and again. And the ground at our feet reverberated with each deep boom. Behind us, a line of cars was silhouetted on the brow of the hill, each one filled with onlookers.

"Nanny said I could get out to watch as long as I didn't go any further away," Dorothy explained.

There were two people in the open-sided car at our backs. A sweet-faced woman, whose fluffy blonde hair curled from under a close-fitting hat, leaned out and reminded Dorothy, "You haven't introduced your friend, dear. You really mustn't forget your manners."

Dorothy slapped her red-mittened hands to her cheeks and laughed with delight. "Nanny," she said. "This is the girl I was telling you about. Wren, this is Nanny. She's really Miss Ames, but she's been Nanny to me since I was two."

The car's other occupant was the driver, a

young woman with silver-blond hair, held flat by a ribbon of black velvet which encircled her head. She had small, even features and startling eyebrows drawn on a white complexion. The contrast between her glamour and Miss Ames' natural prettiness was striking. She was buried to her chin in a lustrous gray fur collar that blew softly in the wind, caressing her cheeks. I couldn't help staring. I was sure she was a movie star.

"This is Miss Sadie Moore," said Dorothy's nanny, continuing the introductions. "Wren is a new friend of Dorothy's, Miss Moore. She lives here in Trenton."

"Ah, one of the natives," drawled Miss Moore, stretching a limp, gloved hand over the car door in my direction. "Charmed, I'm sure."

"Ooh," cried Dorothy as another explosion burst over our heads and she ducked down, pretending to be frightened. "That was a close one." She pulled me away then, around to the back of the car, where we could huddle together, out of earshot.

"Is that lady someone famous?" I whispered.

"Not yet. But Daddy has promised her she will be. Do you know Mr. Burton Howard, the famous American film star? He came to see Daddy last week. He had his secretary with him. That was

Miss Moore. Just as soon as Daddy saw her, he decided she had to have a part in his picture. Isn't she just the most beautiful woman you ever saw?"

I looked back at the elegant, bleached hair above the furs.

"Of course, she's not really Mr. Howard's secretary," Dorothy smiled knowingly.

"Who is she, then?" I asked.

"His paramour, silly."

"You mean, his girlfriend?"

"Of course. He just tells people she's his secretary to explain why they're always together. But I know. Daddy says I don't miss much."

It had started to rain, and what had begun as a fine, drizzling mist that clung to our hair soon became a steady downpour which soaked into the shoulders of Dorothy's woollen coat. Another explosion burst from the hillside below us. Dorothy clapped her hands over her ears. "What was that?" I asked.

"Isn't the noise frightful? I hope you aren't afraid. Those aren't real bombs, you know. Daddy said they're made of stumping powder. Someone buries it, and when it's lit, it goes off, blowing dirt into the air, just like a bomb being dropped."

"They look real enough," I agreed.

"Oh, they have to, absolutely," said Dorothy. "This is a very important scene Daddy's filming today. The battlefield scene."

Another explosion below us caused a sudden flurry of activity. A group of a dozen soldiers surged up out of a trench of mounded earth and rushed forward, two or three of them staggering and crumpling into the mud, as if hit by shells fired from guns somewhere out of sight. The crowd on the hill cheered, the cameras rolled, and the rain fell around us in wet sheets.

That same scene, or one very much like it, was re-enacted for the cameras two or three times more. Dorothy clapped and stamped her feet, as delighted as the rest of the onlookers. Then, for the moment, the action seemed to be over. The spectators waited anxiously for several minutes, getting wetter all the time, but nothing else happened. Instead, the dead and wounded soldiers scrambled to their feet and joined comrades and enemies alike to seek shelter under a makeshift canopy beside a large truck.

We hopped from one chilly foot to the other, breathing clouds of vapour and waiting. "Oh, you can't be finished yet! Please, please, please," Dorothy begged.

But there were no more explosions, and with some hesitancy at first, in spite of the dismal weather, the crowd on the brow of the hill started to scatter. After a few minutes, the truck made its way up over the rough ground towards us, the back of the vehicle filled with soldiers clinging to the sides.

"What a pity! I guess the rain has finished Daddy's filming for today." People began to straggle back up the road and several of the cars drew away. "Oh, Wren. I hope you aren't too disappointed. Daddy's been having the most awful time getting this scene filmed. All the snow we've been getting this week has slowed things down. This morning the fire department had to come with their hoses to wash it all away. I wanted to cry because I just love the snow, but there isn't supposed to be any on the ground in the script."

The truck had reached the road and heaved off towards town, gears grinding. "I really can't see what fun that would be for anyone, can you?" Dorothy asked, watching the retreating load of movie extras. "All the mud. Their costumes are absolutely filthy."

"I guess they'd go through just about anything to be in a movie," I reasoned, wiping the wet hair back from my eyes. "Besides, my Gramps told me a lot of them need the work."

Miss Ames was calling us from the car. "I think

you girls had better get inside. You'll both be soaked right through."

Dorothy hurried forward. "We don't have to go back yet, do we, Nanny? Wren just got here."

"I see your father coming, dear. You don't mind waiting, do you, Miss Moore?" she asked of their driver. "Just until I hear what he has to say?"

"Come on, Wren. Get inside," Dorothy urged. "Maybe Daddy'll take us down the hill to see where they were shooting. You can't get too close while they're filming these battle scenes, but they're done now, so Daddy will show us. I just have to ask him."

I climbed into the back seat with her, glad to escape the freezing rain. "You need to have side curtains for this car, Sadie," Dorothy informed her.

Head down, dressed in a bulky overcoat, scarf and rubbers, Donald Donaldson strode across the rough track worn in the matted grass to the edge of the road. Surrounded by an entourage, all shouldering heavy camera equipment or lights, he was unaware of our presence.

"Daddy! Daddy! It's me!" Dorothy cried, her head out the side of the car.

Donaldson stopped abruptly. The frown on his face deepened as he approached the car. "I didn't expect to see you here, my dear," he said. His disapproving gaze was reserved for his daughter's nanny. Miss Moore he acknowledged with a quick lift of his cap. I didn't think he even noticed me.

"You don't mind, do you, Daddy?" Dorothy asked. "Miss Moore wanted to see the location, and she invited Nanny and me to come along in her car."

Mr. Donaldson forced a weary smile. "Perfectly fine, my dear. I'm just sorry I can't join you ladies. But I have work to do back at the studio. This wretched weather has ruined another day of shooting for me. Once again I've had to tell the extras to go home."

"Mr. D.! Mr. D.!" A man wearing a fur coat so long he was tripping over it hurried towards us. "The shooting schedule for tomorrow?" he gasped, his breath visible on the chill air. "May I talk to you about it, Mr. D?"

Mr. Donaldson held a big hand up, halting the man's advance like a traffic cop while he spoke into the car. "Have Michaels bring Miss Moore to the studio first thing in the morning, Nanny," he directed.

"Of course, sir."

"Now, I must be off."

He had taken several paces away from the car when suddenly he stopped, seemed to remember something, and came back towards us again, his coat whipping around him in the wind. "What did you say your name was?" he asked, looking directly at me.

I gulped. "I . . . I didn't say, sir."

"She's Wren, Daddy, remember?" Dorothy burbled happily. "My new friend?"

"Ah, yes. Of course." He tucked the ends of his long scarf down inside his coat, buttoning it again. "Well, Wren," he began, leaning into the car and smiling warmly, taking me totally by surprise. "How would you like to be in my picture?"

Chapter 7

I was so thunderstruck that for a moment I couldn't think of a single thing to say. Dorothy was bouncing up and down in excitement on the seat beside me. The two women in the front, who must have been as startled by Mr. Donaldson's question as I was, had both turned around to watch my face.

Dorothy finally broke the open-mouthed silence. "Really, Daddy? Ooh, Wren. Isn't this wonderful?" She squeezed my arm so hard that it hurt.

"It's just a small part, my dear," Mr. Donaldson said. "Could you step down from there a minute?" He took his foot off the running board, opened the car door and stepped back to let me stumble out onto the wet gravel. "Just stand there, would you, and let me have a good look at you."

He kept nodding his head as he circled me

slowly. "You certainly have the right look about you." He wasn't put off by my drowned rat appearance. The chocolate stains on the front of my purple and fuschia ski jacket, my oldest pair of Saturday jeans, and my scuffed and sodden sneakers didn't seem to matter to him.

"Would you care to do it?" Mr. Donaldson asked, his big hands covering his ears against the wind. "We're shooting the scene almost immediately. It shouldn't take too long."

Almost immediately was best for me too. As long as I was here anyway. "I've never been in a movie before," I admitted. "Except for the home videos my dad takes." Little shivers of excitement seized me. Just wait till Dawn hears about this, I thought.

"Good show," enthused Mr. Donaldson. "I'll get Michaels to take you around to the property shop right away. Tell the wardrobe mistress it's for the part of one of the French farm children. I'm sure she'll have something in your size. Oh, and plaits for your hair, please."

"Plaits?"

Donaldson snapped his fingers at the unhappy man in the big fur coat who was still waiting in the drizzle to speak to him. "Have my chauffeur bring the car here at once," he ordered.

"Now, child." He laid a hand on my shoulder and crouched down in the rain beside me. His voice took on the tender tone I'd heard him use only with Dorothy. "I'll tell you a little about what I need from you. There's a scene in a French village where the soldiers come for a bit of rest and relaxation. Most of the action centres around the Three Ducks Café, but there are some shots of the neighbouring farms.

"It's an indoor set, so we can do it now while we wait for the weather to clear. You'll be herding geese across the square in front of the café with the other children in the first scene. You're not afraid of geese, are you?"

I didn't think so. I didn't know much about geese, except that they flew honking over our house in ragged Vs after the ice was gone from the Bay of Quinte each spring, and that we heard them again around Thanksgiving, headed in the opposite direction. "I love geese," I said fervently.

"Splendid," Mr. Donaldson exclaimed. "Now then, your biggest part comes later in the script. We might use you as one of the youngest members of the family which saves the life of a wounded soldier. What do you say?"

I could feel my grin growing wider by the minute. Oh, please don't snap me back to the

1990s before this part ends, I prayed. "I'd really love it," I replied.

"Right. That's the spirit." Another car pulled up behind us. "Here's Michaels now," said Mr. Donaldson. "When you've got your costume, come to the studio."

"Can I go too, Daddy? Please?" Dorothy begged.

"Go along for the ride, my dear, of course. But Michaels will take you back home after he drops your friend off. Nanny will be waiting for you."

The two of us abandoned Nanny and Sadie Moore to clamber into the long, black car whose open door awaited us. "Phooey!" muttered Dorothy as she flopped against the plush upholstery inside. "Someone's always taking me home!"

The man called Michaels closed the door and slid behind the ivory coloured steering wheel. He had fair hair, a small mustache, and he smiled at Dorothy's exasperation. I liked him right away. There were no seat belts in the car, and I perched on the very edge of the seat, unable to keep my eager feet from tapping on the floor.

"Michaels is sweet on Nanny," Dorothy announced in a loud voice. "They think I don't know, but, as Daddy says, I don't miss much."

I watched Michaels' back for a sign that he

had heard. His shoulders in the immaculate uniform remained relaxed, his gloved hands steady on the wheel.

It was only a short drive back into the city from the location of the battle scene. We drew up in front of a row of houses on a familiar residential street, and Michaels got out smartly. "Here you are, Miss," he said.

"Is this it?" Dorothy peered out the side of the car and wrinkled her nose. "It can't be. It looks like someone's house."

"It was, Miss. The company took over three of the houses on this street." Michaels swung the door wide. "Shall I see you in, Miss?" A group of young men dressed as soldiers, guns over their shoulders, passed us, jostling and laughing, and headed up the street. Michaels reached automatically for my hand.

"Wren! Wren!" Dorothy called from the car. "Tell me all about it the next time I see you."

"I will," I promised.

The house at the end of the path was bursting with noisy people. The inside must have been full because quite a few had spilled onto the front porch where they perched on the railings or squatted on the steps. Since bodies filled the doorway and there was no way anyone could get the door shut, it stayed open in spite of the chill.

"That's okay, Michaels," I assured him as I joined the crowd at the foot of the steps. "I'll be fine, thanks. I can find my way from here, and besides, there's not room for both of us in there."

"Best of luck then, Miss." The chauffeur touched his finger to his cap.

As the car drove off, I threaded my way though the mob on the porch and managed to squeeze inside. How, I wondered, was I ever going to find the person in charge of costumes?

"You are just going to have to wait your turn!" someone shouted over the racket. "Please don't push. I would suggest some of you go out into the back yard. Please."

The speaker was a red-faced woman with a tape measure around her neck and dozens of straight pins stuck through the front of her blouse. This had to be the wardrobe mistress. She had climbed up onto a chair in order to command everyone's attention. "I'd like to get the uniforms out of the way first. British soldiers, please. This way. Everyone else, step aside."

There was some small rearrangement of bodies in the room. It didn't make much difference, and it didn't look like I was going to be waited on for a while, so I did as I was told and worked my way out through what had been the kitchen to a rear door and stepped down into the small yard. Now I had a chance to look around.

Someone's former garden shed sported a sign over the door which read "Carpentry Shop". Everything had been something else before.

I edged through another group of people standing inside the doorway of the shed, out of the cold mist, and watched a man painting scenery. He was adding charred beams to a backdrop of a bombed out church, its stained glass windows shattered, its furnishings upturned or broken to pieces.

"Are you in the movie?" a voice behind me asked suddenly, making me jump. I turned to see a tall girl, eating an apple. She had a mane of wavy red hair, parted on one side and clipped with a plastic barrette. The sweater pulled over her floral cotton dress was too thin and too badly shrunken to be warm.

"I guess so," I smiled. "Mr. Donaldson told me to come and get a costume. He thinks I could play one of the French farm children."

"M-m-m, lucky," remarked the girl, taking another bite of the apple and licking the juice that ran down her chapped wrist.

"Are you in it, too?" I asked.

"Not yet," the girl replied. "But I'm going to be. I read in the newspaper back in Montreal about them needing extras. Took all my savings and came down here by train."

"That's a long way to come when you weren't sure of a part," I said.

"Oh, I'll get the part," she said. "They're looking for lots of us to play farm women and saloon girls. How'd you get picked?"

"Mr. Donaldson saw me with his daughter," I replied. "We're sort of friends."

The girl sniffed. "My, wasn't that a piece of luck!"

The man painting scenery spoke without turning around. "It's his missus who has the final say. If her ladyship likes the look of you, you're in." He dipped his brush into a pail of black paint and wiped the excess on the rim.

"That's what they tell me too," the girl agreed mournfully.

"I'd better go back in and see if I can get my costume now." I stepped around the redhead. "I don't have a lot of time."

The crowd inside had thinned out a little, but not by much. Every available inch of space in the house seemed to be covered with props—from candlesticks and bagpipes to rifles and bayonets, every surface piled high. I stood behind a young man being outfitted in an army uniform.

"But look, Ma'am," he complained, looking down at his feet. "These boots are three sizes too big."

"They'll fit someone else if they don't suit you," was the wardrobe mistress' retort. "And you, dear?" She was talking to me, pushing at the pile of hair that kept falling over her moist forehead.

"Mr. Donaldson told me to tell you a French farm girl?"

"Really? Mr. D?" She raised her ragged eyebrows for an instant and then reached around to draw a peasant blouse from the rack of costumes behind her. "I'm sure he knows what he's doing. Skirt will be enormous on you, though."

"Hold on there a minute!" A heavy-set woman in a fitted navy coat and matching, veiled hat stepped forward. The dotted veil failed to cover the unpleasant look on her face. "I don't know what he could be thinking," she declared, and she seized the outfit from the wardrobe mistress before I could get to it. My jaw dropped at the woman's rudeness.

"Your husband told this child to come in, Ma'am." The wardrobe mistress was trying to ease the clothing away from the other woman.

I shut my mouth. So this was Dorothy's mother. The only one of the family I hadn't met.

She glared at me. "You won't do at all," she declared flatly, sizing me up with a chilly once-over. The wardrobe mistress merely shrugged.

"She's much too young," Mrs. Donaldson went on. "Almost anyone else would do." She looked swiftly around at the others. "Here, even this one." And she yanked the girl I'd met in the back yard through the stunned group which had clustered around us. "She's more like it."

"Me?" the redhead blinked.

"Yes, you. You come along with me."

"Where to?"

"To the studio, of course. My car's outside."

"She's Donaldson's wife," someone hissed, giving the redhead a shove.

As quickly as she had appeared, Mrs. Donaldson whirled out of the house with the girl in tow, slamming the front door so decisively behind them that the window panes rattled.

"Too bad, squirt," remarked the boy in the enormous boots. "They say she's the boss."

"She didn't even give me a chance," I said lamely.

"I only do as I'm told," the wardrobe mistress complained. She gave a helpless gesture with her hands and turned to pull another rack of costumes to the front. She had work to do. "Next?"

"Come on down to the studio with us anyway," the boy invited with a wink. "It won't hurt. People have been known to change their minds. Even old D.D."

The front door opened again, just a crack, and a familiar face appeared around it. "Wren?" It was Dorothy, and behind her was Miss Ames, looking apologetic. They both slipped inside. "I begged Nanny to let me come back," Dorothy explained, coming over to me and slipping her arm through mine. "And now Mummy has taken Michaels and our car to the studio."

"We'll just wait here until they get back," Nanny said in her soft voice. "Come, Dorothy. We'll find a place to sit down."

"I had the part, Dorothy," I whispered hoarsely. "Your father said I could have the part. Then your mother came and picked someone else. Just like that."

"I'm sorry, Wren," said Dorothy.

Nanny had managed to find some space on the other side of the room, on a bench just vacated by the last happy group to leave for the studio. I dropped onto it, heavy with misery. "I don't know how anyone could be so mean."

"Oh, Mummy isn't mean," Dorothy said,

earnestly. "She's a very good judge of talent. Daddy trusts her absolutely."

I said nothing. Tears of disappointment pricked at my eyes. To keep from crying, I studied the worn spots on the brown linoleum at my feet, ignoring the people still jamming themselves into the house. I might as well wake up right now, I thought; the best part of my dream is over anyway.

Suddenly my mind snapped to attention. "The costumes for the ballroom scene?" I heard a male voice over the constant babble.

I got quickly to my feet to see who the speaker might be, but he was hidden from me, standing on the other side of the open door.

"No costumes, except for the stars," the wardrobe mistress stated. "It says here you are expected to provide your own. Formal evening wear. Can you get something?"

Frantically, I pushed my way back into the throng, ignoring Dorothy's plucking fingers. By the time I reached the door, it had shut again and I was trapped by the crowd. From the window I could see the backs of two people, a sandy-haired man and a slim woman, walking away from the house. The man took the woman's hand, and they turned to the right as they reached the street out the front. Could it have been them, I wondered? Could I have come that close to seeing my grandparents?

I leaned over the counter, grabbing at the wardrobe mistress to get her attention. "The ballroom scene," I begged. "Do you know where they're filming it?"

"The Morrison House Hotel is what they told me," she replied. "I'm not sure of the schedule yet. A week from now, I think they said. But darling, you are definitely much too young for that one."

Dorothy was at my elbow again. "It's an indoor set," she whispered. "You can't just go and watch it."

"Are you sure? Oh, Dorothy, there must be a way."

She fingered the buttons on her coat, her eyes downcast. "Well, maybe I could get Daddy to let us. He'll usually do anything for me."

"Do you think he'll do this?"

Her forehead wrinkled in concern. "Would it make up for what happened here today?"

I wanted to hug her. "Oh, Dorothy. It really would!"

"Then I'll just ask him." She stuck out her little chin. "I'll find out when they are filming it, and we'll go and watch it together." Nanny was signaling to us, making pointed gestures at the bench beside her.

"How will you let me know?" I asked as we forced our way back across the crowded room.

Dorothy turned to face me with a fervent promise. "I'll leave a message for you," she said.

Relieved, I sat down again. I let my head fall back against the tattered wallpaper behind the bench. The sudden rush of excitement, followed by the crash of bitter disappointment, left me feeling drained and tired. All I wanted to do now was lie down and think about the afternoon's events. The scene around me began gradually to blur, the chatter of eager voices faded away, and I found myself back in my own room.

I lay still and listened for familiar sounds in the house, and then I remembered that the family had gone shopping. Leaving my bed, I went to look in the mirror. A single face gazed back at me—my own—and the backwards letters behind me on the Xanadu poster.

I'd come so close.

Chapter 8

In the days which followed, I begrudged even a single minute spent away from the mirror. If I weren't there when she appeared, how would Dorothy leave me a message? And what kind of a message would it be? I wasn't worried that anyone else in the family would intercept it. I was still the only one who had been able to see more than her own reflection in the glass.

I told no one that Donald Donaldson had actually wanted me in his film. I knew even Dawn would have trouble accepting the notion that, had it not been for Mrs. Donaldson, I too would have been in the movie. A likely story!

On the day that I went with Mom and the twins to put up Gramps' Christmas decorations, he had another visitor there by the time we arrived. An elderly man sat in the upholstered rocker in the warm kitchen, stroking Gramps' cat, which lay curled contentedly in his lap.

"This here's a friend of mine, Billy Walters," Gramps introduced his visitor. Billy Walters was the thinnest man I'd ever seen, his forehead and cheek bones prominent under a covering of shiny skin. His head was totally bald and reflected the light of the lamp behind his chair.

"Now, Billy's someone who can tell you all about that famous Englishman and his big war picture," Gramps declared. "He had a pretty big part in the movie. So I thought, who better to help you with that school project of yours, Wren."

"My part wasn't that big," Billy protested in a voice so hollow that my sisters tried to smother mischievous giggles at the sound of it.

Eagerly, I slung my jacket over the coat rack and settled down in front of Billy Walters. "So, how did you get a part in Mr. Donaldson's movie?" I asked. Could I have seen him as a young man, one of the extras waiting in line for a costume?

"I just heard they were hiring extras," Billy said. "And a bunch of us went to the property shop and they gave us all uniforms. I played the part of a British soldier." (Maybe he was one of the soldiers I had seen!) "They must have thought I was pretty good because they put a balaclava over my head, and I got to play the part of a German soldier in another scene."

"This is so cool," I enthused. "I want to hear all about it."

"You'll have to excuse Wren, Mr. Walters," said Mom, dislodging me from the footstool at his feet where I had parked myself. "She has to learn to listen while she works." And she handed me a string of coloured lights to untangle. The twins were still dragging boxes of decorations out of the hall closet.

Although Gramps no longer put up a Christmas tree, every year we tried to make his house look "Christmassy". He always told us it lifted his spirits to see all the old decorations again.

"Where to begin," said Billy Walters, seeing that we were all at work now, but casting expectant glances in his direction. "Well, the Studio was here already, built in 1917. I guess Donaldson came up this way one time while he was visiting New York. He fell in love with the place, they say. He considered the scenery around here perfect for his movie. He liked the area out on the edge of town especially, said the long rows of poplar trees reminded him of parts of France. He'd served in the war too, belonged to a British regiment."

"Told you he knew all about it," said Gramps proudly, sitting down and taking an egg carton of ornaments onto his lap. "Now me, I was too busy unloading coal off the lake boats down at the town docks. Till my sweetheart persuaded me it was a way to make an extra dollar or two."

"So how was it then?" I pressed. "Being in the movies?"

"Oh, it was great fun for a youngster like me," Billy Walters replied. "Running here and there with fixed bayonet, dressed up like a soldier. What I remember most though, was all the mud. It was something terrible. It rained practically every day we were shooting."

"I know," I said, and when they all turned to look at me, I shrugged. "I read how awful the weather was that year."

Billy Walters nodded. "That's the kind of weather we get here in November. When it doesn't rain, it snows. Worse still is the sleet. Someone should have warned Donaldson. He'd gone and hired all those extras, and then he kept having to send them home.

"As for the big-time movie stars he'd brought in from the States, sometimes they hung around town for days on end, doing nothing except piling up bills. Terrible waste of money. We used to say old Donaldson would tear out the last of his hair before the movie was finished. He didn't have much, you know. Always wore a cap, indoors and out, kind of like his trademark, you might say." Gramps' cat kept up a rhythmic purring while Billy stroked her and talked on.

"Every day of delay meant his mood went from bad to worse. It's a wonder he had anyone left who would work for him. And in the end the wonderful dream died. The tradespeople in town were left with a bad taste in their mouths when Donaldson went back to England owing so many of them money."

"Don't be too hard on Donaldson," Gramps spoke up, handing me a painted ornament from the box and watching critically while I held it up to the window for his approval. "I think that one would be better over the sink," he suggested. "I always figured it must have been pretty rough trying to make a movie with as many amateurs as he had."

"He couldn't afford to pay for anything else," Billy countered.

"Maybe not," Gramps said. "But the men who backed him in the business, I heard later, lost interest in the picture once it was made. No one ever got to see it in the States or Great Britain. They pulled the rug out from under him."

Billy agreed. "True enough. The rights to the movie were never sold to the Americans. That meant certain doom."

"Is that why they stopped making movies here?" I wondered. "Gramps told me Donald Donaldson's company wasn't the only one using the Studio."

"No, but 'talkies' came in after that," Billy explained. "All the lab equipment at the Trenton studio was out of date, cost too much to change it."

"So all we have left is the building, and now we can't even use that," I said.

"On that gloomy note," Mom interrupted, "let's try these lights. Can you reach the plug, Genevieve?"

My sister wriggled on hands and knees underneath the china cabinet, and in a moment the small kitchen was bathed in warm, coloured light. Gramps and his old friend nodded approvingly. "Mighty nice, I'd say. Mighty nice." Gramps' voice was soft. "I always think of Nettie when I see all her Christmas things."

Standing behind Gramps, Mom wrapped her arms around him, chair and all. "And to think you didn't want to bother," she teased.

"It wasn't all bad though, was it, Mr. Walters?" I asked, remembering the excitement I'd witnessed in the property shop, the eager faces of the people waiting for a chance to be in the movies.

"Oh, by no means was it all bad. You ever hear the term 'Hollywood North?' That's what they called Trenton back then. It was great. Something we old codgers will never forget. Besides, who knows? If the picture had been a roaring success, I might have left this town and would be lying today under a palm tree somewhere with the rich and famous."

That was an image I had trouble picturing.

"Hardly your style, Billy," declared Gramps. "But that's exactly what happened to Deanna Dundas, isn't it? Some Hollywood studio saw her and signed her to a big contract."

"Oh, I remember her," cried Mom. "She was still a big name when I was growing up."

"She was nobody before Donaldson's movie," said Gramps.

"What about Sadie Moore?" I had to know. "I read that she was in it."

"Never heard of her again," Gramps frowned, and Billy shook his head. "Me neither."

"But Deanna Dundas, or that was what they changed her name to later, she was a beauty, a redhead from Montreal. She owed her career to this picture."

"Yep, she made it big, all right," Billy agreed. The cat leapt off his lap then, landing soundlessly and giving a luxurious stretch.

I picked up the leftover decorations and nestled them carefully back in the boxes, folding the flaps down to close the top. So Dorothy's mother had been right about the girl. Maybe she had been a good judge of talent after all.

Mom lifted some plates down from the cupboard and began to prepare a snack for us, slicing cheese and opening the box of crackers she'd brought with her.

Billy Walters abandoned his rocking chair for a seat at the table as soon as he spied the food. "Do you remember, Ed?" he asked. "When the movie came to town? The Odeon was packed for every showing. We'd all jump up and holler every time the smoke cleared on the screen and we saw ourselves up there." He bit into a cheese and cracker sandwich with long teeth, scattering crumbs onto the tablecloth. "But we never found you and Nettie, did we?"

Gramps set a square of yellow cheese onto a round cracker. "Nope. We went a couple of times too, to see it. I'm afraid we ended up 'on the cutting room floor,' as they say. But I do remember we had to go to the Morrison House for the filming of the scene we were in. December, it was, 1927. And we were married the next spring." His cracker hovered halfway to his mouth, forgotten as he reminisced. "No wonder she was able to talk me into it."

"You do know how to put on a nice lunch, Mrs. Ferris," said Billy happily.

Mom patted his bony hand. "You were hungry, weren't you, dear? Wren, you save that last pickle for Mr. Walters."

Chapter **9** **9** ɹǝʇdɐɥƆ

The wardrobe mistress had said the ballroom scene might be filmed the very next week. Time was passing and still I hadn't heard from Dorothy. The fear that I might miss the shooting of that scene, the only one my grandparents had been in, was almost more than I could bear. Surely, Dorothy had understood how important it was to me. Surely by now she knew the time of the shoot. Why hadn't she let me know?

I sat glued to the desk in my room, hoping against hope that sheer will power would cause Dorothy's serious little face to appear in the mirror. But hard as I tried to see that in my mind, the only thing behind me remained the familiar poster, the artist's impression of Kubla Khan's stately pleasure dome and the winding river, shrouded in mystic clouds of pink. The words of the verse I knew by heart, backwards and forwards. "In Xanadu did Kubla Khan a stately pleasure dome decree . . ."

It was odd how some of the letters, although backwards, stood out from the rest of the script. I'd never noticed that before. They had a three-dimensional quality to them. I peered more closely at the letters in the mirror. They were jumping right out at me!

I wrote down the ones which stuck out, in the order they appeared in the poem. Could this be Dorothy's message? XAMDECELEVEN.

"It doesn't make sense," I muttered, sounding out the letters. I fiddled with them, separating them, and almost at once the last part of the message became clear. "Deceleven. Dec. eleven. December eleven. Tomorrow!

"But Xam? Would you pronounce it Zam, which rhymes with Jam?" But it was an X. X, that was the Roman numeral for ten. Of course! Ten a.m., December eleventh! It just had to be from Dorothy!

Tomorrow at ten o'clock I would be waiting. Tomorrow was Sunday. Perfect. No school, so I could be ready the instant Dorothy appeared.

❧ ❧ ❧

"Of course you can't stay home," my mother insisted. "This is something we do every year."

"But does it have to be tomorrow?" I pleaded.

"Don't be ridiculous, Wren," Mom said. "Of course, it's tomorrow. Everyone else will be there tomorrow, so that's where we will be too. You know we work together on this. All of us."

I tried to reason with her. "I don't know why you need me. With so many other people there to help."

"This is a family thing, Wren. And this is the season of giving, in case you've forgotten."

This conversation wasn't getting me anywhere. Of one thing only I was certain, that the annual Ferris family event of helping to pack the holiday food hampers at the community centre would not keep me from meeting Dorothy at the appointed time.

"Let's be reasonable about this," Dad said, setting his fork down. He had been listening to Mom and me arguing all through supper. "Why can't you go, Wren?"

"I just have too much homework to do. My history project is due right after the holiday."

"There'll be plenty of time to do that when school gets out," Mom insisted. She was right, of course, but I couldn't tell them the real reason. Then there'd be no way I'd get out of going with them.

"You aren't being very nice, Wren," said

Genevieve in a self-righteous tone.

This couldn't be happening. I absolutely could not miss the filming of the ballroom scene. Everything else paled in importance beside it. I even considered pretending I was sick, faking illness so that I could stay home when the others left.

Saturday night I crawled into bed with the problem still unresolved, my mind in turmoil. How was I going to get out of this family thing? I just had to be right here at ten o'clock the next morning.

I tossed and turned for what seemed the entire night. I was sure I never slept, but if not, when did I dream such desperate dreams? In one, my mother, filled with the best of intentions as she always was, had taken my mirror away somewhere to be re-finished. I awoke in a sweat and leapt up out of bed to touch the cool glass. It was still there.

I slept again. Sometime towards dawn, Dorothy appeared in a nightmare, trapped inside the mirror, pressing her hands against its surface, frantically mouthing words I couldn't hear.

Then it was morning. I had not come up with a solution to my dilemma and, filled with resentment, I clomped downstairs and out to the car where the others were waiting. I'd left a message in lipstick letters on the mirror for Dorothy. "I will be here at 10. Please wait. W." I was just going to have to escape somehow. I'd emptied my piggy bank of all its contents, prepared to bribe someone for a ride home, if necessary.

At the community centre, the usual mountain of cans and boxes awaited us, the usual sea of noise. The entire main floor had been taken over by food and people. There were people with lists, people sorting into hampers, children running here and there, everyone carrying in more plastic bags and boxes from the grocery stores.

One of Mom's friends met us at the door. "I knew we could count on you folks to help us out. What a mad house!" she babbled happily. "Isn't it wonderful? You know, the response is so good this year that once we get all these hampers filled, there's going to be enough left over to stock the shelves at the food bank. I just can't believe it. Come on girls, I'll show you what needs doing."

My job was to separate the tins of baked beans from the other canned goods on one of the tables. I watched the clock on the wall. The minute hand moved every 60 seconds with little jerks that I could almost feel. How was I going to get out of here?

Unwittingly, it was my own mother who provided the chance to escape. I'd been sorting for nearly an hour, getting more frantic with every minute, when she came by, mopping her brow. "I think I must have left that case of macaroni and cheese in the trunk of the car," she said. "Do you think you could get it, dear? If you find it's too heavy for you to carry, I'll hunt up your father."

Never have I been so quick to respond. "I can get it, Mom. I helped you put it in, remember?"

"Just take it over to Mrs. Rubecki, then. She's in charge of the carbohydrates." She hurried away, her mind already on the next task as she called, "Jennifer, this hamper here has no peanut butter in it, dear."

"Where to, little lady?" the driver asked as I tumbled into the back seat of the taxi, keeping my head down, out of sight of anyone entering or leaving the community centre. "1234 Edgeview Crescent," I gasped, just like in the movies. "And please hurry!"

At the house, I fished the front door key out of the window box and took the stairs to my room, two at a time. Ten-twenty already. I flung myself into the chair in front of the mirror. Nothing.

After a couple of minutes, I raced into the bathroom for some paper towels, returning to wipe my lipstick message off the glass.

Unzipping my jacket, I sat down again to wait, praying I hadn't missed her, praying that Dorothy would still come. And before my mother discovered I'd never returned with the case of macaroni and cheese for Mrs. Rubecki.

The face that finally swam into focus in the hazy glass was not Dorothy's, but that of her famous father. I swiveled around in my chair. "Mr. Donaldson?"

He had already turned his back and begun to walk away from me. I was on my feet at once. The walls of my room receded.

Wherever he was going, Donald Donaldson seemed to be in a great hurry. I crossed a street and followed him right up to the front door of a large building which bore a sign over its front entrance, Morrison House Hotel.

A doorman in a green uniform with brass buttons was greeting a steady stream of people entering through the front door. They were all grown-ups, no sign of Dorothy here. Many of the men wore white scarves knotted elegantly at their throats. Long dresses peeped from under the women's coats. I stood a moment and watched the man with the tarnished braid on his coat touch his cap and hold the heavy glass doors open for each one. No way I was going to be able to get past that doorman, I decided. There must be a back entrance.

I hurried around behind the building to the laneway. A pimply-faced delivery boy of about my age was unloading trays of bread from a horse-drawn wagon at the back door. He grunted as he swung his burden wide to avoid me.

"I'm supposed to be washing dishes here today," I informed him glibly. "Big crowd and everything."

The horse shifted its feet restlessly. "Whoa, now," the boy cautioned, reaching into the back of the wagon for another tray. "Steady, girl."

"They're filming an important scene for Donald Donaldson's movie here today, you know," I said.

"No kidding? Well, you'd better get inside then, squirt." The horse stamped again, its warm breath making clouds in the frosty air. Flooded with relief, I darted past the stack of fragrant bread inside the door and up three steps to the kitchen. I was in!

"Hey! Where are you going?" demanded someone wearing a large, white apron and holding a pot lid in mid-air.

"I'm in the movie," I croaked, caught off guard.

"So, why don't you use the front door like

everyone else?" He turned to set the lid onto a vat of steaming liquid, and I slipped through a swinging door, making my escape.

I had entered a heavily carpeted hallway filled with people who were gathered at the entrance to a large room. I glimpsed ornate wallpaper, chandeliers and high ceilings. The hotel ballroom. On the right, a flight of stairs stretched up to the next floor. Sucking in my breath, I slipped through the crowd and bolted up to the landing where I crouched low, panting to catch my breath.

No one seemed to have noticed me. When I finally felt my racing pulse slow down and I dared to look up, I discovered I had the perfect spot for surveying the scene below. Through the railings of the staircase I could see into part of the ballroom on the main floor. If I slid along the step to the other side, against the wall, I could peer even further into the room.

Donald Donaldson had come in and was perched, tweed cap on his head, on a folding chair just inside the door, behind the spotlights. The elegantly dressed figures I'd seen out front were all circulating about the room now, nodding and talking. The soft clink of glasses and swish of fabric mingled with the low murmur of voices and the whir of the cameras. I wondered where Dorothy was.

Every so often a couple would glide into view before waltzing away again to another part of the room. There didn't seem to be any script for this scene, just a large party of people dancing and mingling, exactly as my grandfather had described it.

After about fifteen or twenty minutes of this, Donaldson stood up. "Enough! Cut!" he ordered. Shaking his head, he strode into the ballroom to arrange people into different clusters, shifting their positions and making suggestions. Back in his chair, he leaned forward and gave directions to the crew again. "Cameras! Action!" Finally, I saw him relax.

I scrutinized each dancing couple, every twosome that visited the punchbowl on the sideboard or leaned in conversation against the mantle of the fireplace, wondering which were my grandparents. Would I recognize Gramps when I saw him? I had never known the woman who had been my grandmother. I wanted to stand up and lean over the railing for a better view, but was afraid of being discovered by someone in the hall below. Why hadn't Dorothy come as she had promised? She at least would have been able to separate the stars from the extras for me.

I recognized Sadie Moore as she made her entrance from the left, sweeping in at Donald Donaldson's cue. She wore a loose, ivory-coloured dress with a long fringe at the knee-length hem which swayed from side to side as she moved. The other "guests" parted to make way for her, while others retreated into the hall, their part in the scene finished.

Suddenly, I spotted them. I knew it had to be them. The sound of my own pulse throbbed in my ears. A slim, sandy-haired man, with a nervous-looking woman on his arm, moved slowly into the hall, out of the eye of the camera. The woman clutched the man's arm with both of her hands. She was a pretty woman with an unlined, delicately freckled face, framed in reddish hair which curled softly against her skin. She could have been my father's younger sister. It was amazing how familiar she looked.

"Cut!" called Donaldson. "That does it, everyone. Thank you."

The couple moved to the foot of the staircase to make room as the others began to crowd out and gather up their coats again. They stood to one side, in no hurry to leave, perhaps wishing to prolong the experience. The man ran a finger inside his collar when he thought no one was looking. The woman who was my grandmother smoothed the fabric of her soft green dress down over her slim hips and smiled to herself.

Suddenly, the man turned and looked directly up to where I was perched. I hadn't moved. What had made him look up? Our eyes met. Something, I don't know what, kinship or something, passed between us. I opened my mouth to speak, no longer afraid of being seen, but no sound came out. The moment passed. I began to shiver.

The man returned his gaze to the young woman. "Did you have fun?" he asked, his voice full of tenderness.

"Oh, yes. It was really exiting, wasn't it, Eddie?" She grabbed his arm again. "Now be honest," she pleaded.

"Well, I suppose it was, my sweet. Yes, it was fun. If it made you happy, then even this collar was worth it."

"You look positively dashing," she said. "I declare, Edgar, you were made to wear evening clothes."

Edgar's laugh was warm. "Even if we can never afford to buy another stitch?"

"You're such a tease, Eddie." The young woman sighed. "But it was all over too fast."

And the scene was over. Most of the extras had already left. My grandfather retrieved their coats, and as he helped his companion into hers, he turned to look up at me again. This time I raised my hand and wiggled my fingers. I knew he wasn't going to tell anyone there was a spy in their midst. "See you in the movies, kid," he said, with a wink. My grandmother must have thought he was talking to her. She gave a tinkly little laugh as she buttoned her coat. They left together by the front door. I remained glued to the stairs.

The technical crew, with lights and cameras, filed out into the hall, packing up to leave. I had to make my own exit fast, before I was spotted by anyone else. But I didn't move quite fast enough.

"My word, Dorothy's little friend!" Donald Donaldson was peering at me through the railing. "What on earth are you doing up there?"

Hastily, I got to my feet, feeling colour flood my face. I was trapped. "I didn't want to miss the filming of this scene," I stammered, coming slowly down the stairs towards him. Would I now feel the fury of his famous temper?

To my surprise, he smiled at me. "If I'd known," he said evenly, "I'd certainly have found you a better seat."

I let out the breath I'd been holding since he first spotted me. "I'd hoped to meet Dorothy here, sir," I explained. "We thought we'd watch the filming together. But she never came."

"Oh no, my dear. How could she?" He rested both his hands, one on top of the other, on the newel post. "She has gone back home. To England."

"She has? I mean, she didn't even say good-bye. Dorothy asked me to come today. I didn't know she'd be going back to England."

"I didn't know, either," Mr. Donaldson admitted, and the sadness in his eyes was evident. "It's this dampness. My wife thinks it may be making her headaches worse. She's been in agony, you know, practically the whole time she's been here."

"I'm sorry," I said lamely. I'd heard the weather was pretty damp in England most of the time, but didn't mention it. "Will Dorothy be back after the holidays then? You aren't finished the movie yet, are you?"

"Dorothy will be returning to her school in England, I'm afraid," her father said. "She will not be coming back here. As for the crew, we're doing some indoor shooting in Kingston next, at the locomotive works there." He sounded less than enthusiastic. "I'm praying for good weather to finish up in Canada by early spring. Then we can all go home. This just has not worked out as well as I'd hoped." He was holding the door of the hotel open for me. I saw the doorman, still in his costume, walking away up the street.

Mr. Donaldson sighed and adjusted his cap more firmly on his head. "We're leaving tonight for Kingston, so I must say good-bye now, my dear." I took the hand he extended. "I'll tell Dorothy when I see her that you asked about her. Hurry along, now."

Obediently, I began to walk away from him. I looked back over my shoulder once, but everything was beginning to get fuzzy. I stopped to steady myself, more shaken than I realized.

Somewhere someone was pounding loudly at a door. I sat at home in my room, facing the mirror over my desk. I made my way down the stairs to the front door and discovered on the step a big box of groceries and the twins' rotund piano teacher, her hand raised to knock again.

"Am I on time?" Mrs. Obermayer gasped, her face red from exertion. "I told the girls to tell your mother I'd bring something for the food hampers."

My mother! The macaroni!

"I can take this over there myself if I'm too late," the woman offered, probably puzzled by the blank look on my face.

"Actually, you're right on time, Mrs. O.," I

assured her. "The others have gone, but I was looking for a ride to the community centre myself."

No sooner had Mrs. Obermayer dropped me next to our family car, than Dad appeared on the scene. "Oh, there you are, Wren," he said, coming around to where I was fitting the keys into the trunk. "I'm going back for the truck to take some of the leftovers to the food bank. If you're coming with me, run on in and tell your mother. She was wondering where you'd gotten to."

Chapter 10

After saying good-bye to Donald Donaldson at the Morrison House Hotel I saw no more of the faces from the past in the old mirror. Try as I might, I could not conjure up Dorothy's image. It was as if she had indeed left town.

Finally, school let out for the Christmas holidays. But even all the excitement of the festivities at our house could not force me to put the strange happenings of the past few weeks to the back of my mind for more than a moment or two.

Old Mrs. Bain, Mom's client, was spending Christmas Day with us this year, and Dad had brought her over when he'd picked Gramps up from his house. It was the first time I'd seen my grandfather since my encounter with his younger self. I sat across the dinner table from him, studying his eyes, looking for a sign that he remembered what had passed between us in another time. But if I thought we shared a wonderful secret, I was wrong. Gramps looked up to discover me staring at him. "What's the matter?" he demanded. "Do I have cranberry sauce on my chin?"

"Sorry, Gramps. No, there's nothing on your chin." I bent over my plate of roast turkey and trimmings. I had to tell him about it. Sometime, when no one else was around. It didn't even matter that he might not believe it. It was just too special to keep to myself.

My chance came after dinner when Dad had settled his father for a rest on the sofa in the den. Mrs. Bain was content to put her feet up in the living room where she said she would be happy watching the twins playing with the new dollhouse Dad had made for them.

"Would you like me to bring the afghan to cover you?" my father asked at the door to the den.

"I'll get it, Dad," I offered, scrambling to my feet from under the Christmas tree where I'd been arranging a display of the opened presents.

"Thanks, Wren," Dad said. "I'll help your mother load the dishwasher."

Gramps' eyes were closed when I entered the room. "Are you asleep already, Gramps?"

"Just resting my eyes," he said. "No, don't go.

Sit right there and tell me what you've been up to lately."

Eagerly, I pulled the rocking chair over beside him. "I've been dying to tell you, Gramps. It's the most exciting thing."

"It must be," he said dryly, without opening his eyes. "The way you've been twitching all day."

I started at the beginning and told him the whole amazing story. About finding the strange mirror in the movie studio, about buying it and bringing it home, how I'd met Dorothy Donaldson, and how I suddenly found myself transported in time to the year 1927. Gramps listened without interrupting.

I told him about the throng of people gathered outside the Studio the first day I visited it with Dorothy, how everyone was clamoring for parts in the movie, about the way the city had looked back then, about visiting the movie location and meeting Miss Ames, Dorothy's nanny, and the glamourous Miss Sadie Moore, about how close I'd come to being an extra in the film myself. And finally, how I'd gone to the Morrison House to watch the filming of the ballroom scene and to search for my own grandparents there.

Watching the expression on his face, I told him how I'd hidden on the stairs that final day and watched the scene being enacted below me. "Do you remember, Gramps?" I leaned forward, hopefully. "Can you remember seeing me on the stairs? You looked right at me. Then you winked at me and said, 'See you in the movies, kid'."

Gramps' eyes were open and he stared at the ceiling with a faraway look, his lips parted in a small smile. I couldn't tell if his amusement arose from being reminded of the time he and his bride-to-be were in Donald Donaldson's film, or from his granddaughter's fantastic imagination. I waited for him to respond.

"Satin, it was," he mused. "Sea-green, like her eyes."

I slid from the chair and kneeled on the floor beside the couch, level with him. "I was there, Gramps! I saw the two of you. And you saw me. Do you believe such a thing could happen?"

"Well, ordinarily, I wouldn't." He turned gradually onto his right side so that he could look at me and put his hands together beneath his ear. "But when you tell it like that, describing Nettie and how she looked that day, well, that's something I've never forgotten, and I have to believe you saw her too. A picture, she was. And as excited as a little kid. I'd have loved to have gone back there with you, child. All you had to do was ask."

Neither of us spoke for a few moments, and my

grandfather's eyelids closed again, but the smile remained. Now the two of us did share a wonderful secret. Gently, I spread the afghan over him.

"I don't remember a little girl at the Morrison House," Gramps murmured. "I'm sorry about that, child." His eyes were closed, and soon the steady rising and falling of his shoulders indicated that he was asleep. I tiptoed from the room, sure that his dreams would be sweet.

❧ ❧ ❧

On Boxing Day, as I'd done every year for the past three or four, I put some of my favourite Christmas presents into a shopping bag and got ready to go to Dawn's house. It was an unspoken agreement between us that we would compare gifts the day after Christmas was over at our house. I'd already seen her Hanukkah presents, but now I had so much to tell her.

"Can you drop this off at Mrs. Bain's, dear? On your way to Dawn's?" Mom hurried down the steps just as I was leaving, a cardigan sweater over her arm. "She forgot it here yesterday." I laid it on top of my presents in the bag. "And call me when you're ready to come home. If you like, I could pick you up. I have to go out and get some milk anyway."

Tire tracks led out of the Rosen's garage through the thin dusting of snow in the driveway. I pressed the bell at the front door, stamping my feet and waiting, hearing the chimes inside the house. No one was home. I should have phoned first, but Dawn might have known I'd be over. I looked down at the bag of presents, feeling betrayed. Mrs. Bain's blue sweater lay on the top.

At the brick house on the hill, I heard the old lady shuffling slowly towards the door. "You forgot your sweater," I explained, handing it to her.

"And you've come all this way with it. You needn't have, dear. I have other sweaters."

I told her I was in the neighbourhood anyway and that the friend I had intended to visit had not been home.

"Come in, dear," Mrs. Bain invited, opening the door wider. "Such a lovely time I had with you yesterday. It was the best Christmas I've had since my husband passed away. There's nothing so wonderful as a big family."

I was grateful for the warmth of the house and let myself be led inside. "Actually, I was hoping to ask you if I could use your phone to call my mother, Mrs. Bain," I explained. "She said she'd drive me home, and since Dawn was away . . ."

"Of course you may use my telephone. Just put your bag down, and I'll show you where it is."

Off the hall, I caught a glimpse of a living room lined with bookshelves, the walls panelled in dark wood. A curving staircase rose on the right, and beyond it the hallway narrowed. White kitchen appliances gleamed at the other end of the hall. The telephone was on a table in an alcove under the stairs where a small lamp shed soft, yellow light.

Several framed photographs hung on the walls of the alcove. While I listened to the regular beep, beep that indicated that the line at home was busy, I studied the people in the picture frames.

To my surprise, I spotted a familiar face. That man in the photograph, cloth cap set at a jaunty angle. It was Donald Donaldson! Mrs. Bain must have been in his movie. She would be about the right age, I guessed.

"Any luck?" Mrs. Bain inquired from her chair just inside the archway which divided the living room from the hall.

"The line's busy," I said, studying the face behind the glass. "I was looking at this picture over the telephone." I crossed the hall towards her. "It's Donald Donaldson, isn't it? The movie director from England?"

"Yes, of course. How clever of you to recognize it. I have a better picture of him here." She got up, leaning heavily on her cane. Removing a leather-framed photograph from one of the bookcases, she held it out to me. "That one over the phone was his personal favourite. He called it his 'dashing' look."

In this second picture, Donaldson was much older than he had been when I last saw him at the Morrison House; long spine as straight as ever, his huge hands resting on the head of a cane.

"This picture was taken in 1959," said Mrs. Bain. "The year poor Daddy died."

addy?" I felt a chair against the back of my legs and lowered myself onto it. "This man is your father?"

"Of course, dear," Mrs. Bain said, smiling. "I was his only child."

I gulped. "Then, is your name Dorothy?"

Mrs. Bain had returned to her own chair. "That's right."

Dorothy Donaldson. Right here. Right now. In Trenton. This was the little girl who had waited so impatiently for me over the edge of time? This woman with the stooped shoulders, the braid of white hair coiled loosely around her head?

"I thought, when I first saw the picture, that you might have been in the movie he made here," I said when I was able to speak in coherent sentences again.

"Oh, no," Mrs. Bain said. "I was just a child then, dear. But Mother and I were here during the filming."

I didn't know where to begin. It was obvious that Dorothy Bain had not yet made the connection between us. "Did you get to know any of the kids from Trenton when you were here?" I ventured, still looking at the picture I held.

"I'm afraid I led rather a sheltered life," the old lady said. "Nanny was my closest friend, and whenever we went anywhere, Michaels drove us in the car."

I set the leather frame back on the bookcase. "So you didn't meet anyone? No one closer to your own age?"

"Well, actually, there was a child from the town I saw a few times. She was interested in Daddy's film, and we watched some of the shooting together. But then Mother decided rather suddenly that we were going back to England, and I never saw her again. Why do you ask, dear?"

I sat down on the edge of my chair again. "I know who that girl was, Mrs. Bain."

"How could you, dear?"

"It was me. Wren Ferris."

Mrs. Bain frowned. "How could you be that child? Wait a minute. Wren. Yes, I believe that was it. Such an unusual name." Her voice trailed off. "I'm almost seventy-nine years old, dear. It was your grandmother, perhaps?"

"No, not my grandmother. Me. Myself. Have you ever heard of time-travel, Mrs. Bain?"

"Time travel? I've read about it, of course. H. G. Wells and all that. It's purely fiction." She hesitated. "Isn't it?"

"Last November," I began—was it really less than two months ago?—"I was at the old movie studio with my dad. It's going to be torn down, you know. I bought one of the mirrors from the dressing rooms. That's how we met, you and I. I kept seeing you in the mirror. You and your father too. After I learned who you were, I spoke to you one day. It was through the mirror that I was able to go back to 1927, when your father was filming here. And when you were looking for someone your own age to keep you company."

Dorothy Bain was slowly shaking her head from side to side, but a smile was forming at the corners of her mouth.

I seized the opportunity. "Don't you remember? I almost ended up in your father's film myself. He said I could be one of the French farm children, and I even went to get a costume for the part and everything. But then your mother came and said I wouldn't do. You must remember that!"

"I do," she said. "I remember now. You were heart-broken." She put her hands to her cheeks in a gesture that was familiar to me. "It is you, isn't it?" Dorothy started to get up and then sat down again quickly. "Oh, this is all too much. I feel a little dizzy."

"Can I get you anything?" I asked.

She reached for my hand, smiling, reassuring me. "No, dear. I'm all right. But maybe we should have some tea. It is that time, isn't it? And a cup of tea always soothes me."

"I could put the kettle on for you," I offered.

"Would you, dear? The pot's on the counter by the stove, and the tea is in the little canister beside it. And let's have some of those wonderful butter tarts your mother sent home with me." She laid her head back and smiled broadly at me. "Oh, my goodness. What a day!"

I gave Donald Donaldson a satisfied wink as I passed his photograph in the alcove. The events which had tied me to his time in Trenton had gone full circle. The brown velvet eyes seemed to follow me down the hall to the kitchen.

"What happened to Miss Ames?" I asked when I returned to Dorothy's side to wait for the water to boil. "She was so friendly and kind. I loved her right off."

Dorothy seemed to be feeling a little more composed. "Dear Nanny," she sighed. "She married Michaels, the chauffeur. They both stayed on with us for several more years. Then they went to live in the south of England. By that time, they had children of their own. They are both gone now, bless them, but I get a letter from one of their daughters every now and then. Do you know, they had twins in their family, just like yours? I always wished I'd been part of a big family."

After a few minutes I brought in the pot of tea and a plate of my mother's Christmas baking. "The cold weather seems to be making my arthritis worse," Dorothy said, hooking her cane around the leg of a small table and drawing it over beside us. "Just put the tray there, dear. That will be perfect."

I turned the handle of the tea pot towards Dorothy so that she could pour. "You went back to England at Christmastime, in 1927," I said. "So when did you come here again to live?"

"I lived in England for many years," Dorothy explained. "But I married a Canadian airman during the war, and I came to Canada with him after the war was over. After a few years we ended up in Trenton because my husband was stationed here. I was never very good at making friends, and after I discovered there were still some hard feelings about the way Daddy had left things here, I kept pretty much to myself. I had my books to keep me company." She indicated the shelves around the room. "And I never told anyone I had ever been here before. Especially not that I was Donald Donaldson's daughter. Though I'd sometimes wish people could have heard his side of the story."

"I think you'll find things are different now," I said, dropping sugar cubes into my tea. "Maybe you should give people another chance. My Gramps, for one, told me he understood why the movie didn't work out. And he didn't blame Mr. Donaldson." I reached for a tart. "You met my grandfather yesterday. He and my grandmother were extras in the ballroom scene in your father's movie. You two would have a lot to talk about."

"We would, wouldn't we?" Dorothy Bain settled back in her chair, two little spots of pink high on her cheeks. "I think now that perhaps I should have been the one to clear up the misunderstanding." She took a sip of her tea. "Did you know that Daddy put a lot of his own money into the project, and he never received a cent when the picture was finished? Those people who backed his film, they were mostly politicians, and they left him on his own to try to settle with the tradespeople. Of course, I had no idea what was going on. How could I? My mother may have known. Perhaps that's one reason why we left so suddenly. Daddy came back to England a broken man."

I thought how forlorn Mr. Donaldson had looked that last time I saw him, after his family had gone home.

"Poor Daddy was never very good at the financial end of things," Dorothy admitted. "His dream was to make the war movie to end all war movies. And, as sometimes happens with creative people, the little everyday things got neglected. Like who was paying the bills. Daddy woke from his dream to discover that no one was. Perhaps if his backers had stuck by him, and the film had received wider distribution . . ."

She took a determined breath and her smile brightened. "But Daddy got over it. He went on to do some writing for the papers in England. Wrote a book about his experiences, and I think that helped a little. After Mother passed away, he and I became much closer. He wrote a couple of stage plays which received quite good reviews."

She poured a little more tea into her cup and stirred it slowly. "In his later years, Daddy returned to his painting, which gave him great pleasure. Mother never would have approved. She wanted him to be a success in the public's eye."

I saw her give herself a little shake, as if to

clear the unhappy memories. "But now today, imagine seeing my little Canadian friend again. Who would have believed it? And your grandfather speaks kindly of Daddy, you said. I must get your mother to bring him here to visit me. It really is time I made some friends in this city."

❧ ❧ ❧

On the day Mrs. Morrissey handed back the Grade Six local history projects, she held onto mine until all the others had been distributed.

"Top mark goes to Wren Ferris," she announced, beaming at me, "for her project on our city's movie-making industry. Wren, you did a marvelous job. The way you described the filming of the battle scene and the process of hiring extras for the movie, and your detailed diagrams of the various locations, well, it made me feel as if you had been there yourself!

"Class, I'm leaving Wren's project here on the table, and I want every one of you to take a good look at it. Wren has made an important time in Trenton's history come alive."

Before I left school at three-fifteen, I told Mrs. Morrissey that my number one resource for the project had been Donald Donaldson's daughter.

When I told her that Dorothy still lived in Trenton, Mrs. Morrissey invited Mrs. Bain to be the special guest of our class during local history week. That's when things really began to happen.

Before the New Year was two weeks old, my father and I met Mrs. Widdicombe over the frozen food section in the grocery store. "I never thought I'd have to forgive this town for anything worse than wanting to tear down the old Studio," the head of the Heritage Committee declared, "but when I heard that a member of Donald Donaldson's family had been back here in Trenton for years, and almost slipped through our fingers because of ancient hard feelings, that was the last straw!"

She leaned over the freezer, the tone of her voice becoming conspiratorial. "Do you think you could persuade her to address the Heritage Committee at a future meeting, Mr. Ferris?"

"You go ahead and make all the arrangements," Dad promised, dropping a bag of mixed vegetables into our shopping cart and winking at me. "If I can't persuade her, I know a special friend of hers who probably can."

No persuasion was necessary. The next thing we heard, Dorothy Donaldson Bain was negotiating with the city to buy the Studio.

All plans for its demolition ceased.

"I always knew Mrs. Bain was wealthy," Mom said, refolding the local paper one evening and passing it to my dad. "But imagine her doing this for Trenton."

I dropped over the arm of Dad's chair to share with him the story on page one. "Director's Daughter Saves Local Landmark," the headline read. Some minor structural changes would be necessary, but with Mrs. Bain supplying the money, part of the Studio would become a small museum of Canadian film. Dorothy had kept all her famous father's papers and memorabilia, and this would form the basis of the new museum's collection.

The telephone was ringing and I hurried to answer it. It was Dawn, bubbling over with excitement on the other end. "Did you hear the news?" she demanded. "About the Studio?"

"We were just reading about it when you called." I hadn't expected Dawn to be this worked up about it.

"But the best part? Did you get to the best part? About Mom's little theatre group? Mrs. Bain is giving them part of the Studio as a permanent home. Mom's practically ballistic!" It sounded to me as if Dawn were already imagining herself on the road to stardom.

We said good-bye, and gently I set the phone back onto its cradle. I stood for a minute, hearing the murmur of my parents' voices in the living room, the happy chatter of the twins playing upstairs. I gazed out at the lights from the houses across the street, and those which twinkled all the way down to the river and beyond. I thought how grateful this city was going to be for Donald Donaldson's legacy, and I realized how many lives would be different now. And all because of that Saturday last November when I salvaged the old mirror from the Studio.

AUTHOR'S NOTE

This book is a work of fiction. None of its characters ever existed, except in my imagination. Trenton, Ontario is real enough, however, and so is its film-making history. For a few brief years, between 1917 and 1934, it was indeed Hollywood North.

Today, if you visit Trenton, you can read about its movie years on a stone monument the historical society has erected in front of the building which was once the movie studio, on a city street which is still called Film Street.

photo by C. McArthur

As a child, author Peggy Leavey lived in fourteen different localities in Canada, but after marrying, she settled in Trenton, Ontario, where she raised a family and where she still lives. She is a public librarian and has written several books on local history, as well as many newspaper and magazine articles. *A Circle in Time* is her second novel for children. The first was *Help Wanted: Wednesdays Only* (Napoleon 1994).